THE LAVENDER FIELDS

By
Derek Mola

Cover Art: Matteo Gallo
Editor: Nicholas Carter
Illustrator: Kayleigh Sorrentino
Book Layout Design: Stepheniebrown042@gmail.com

ISBN:
(Print) 979-8-218-48514-6
(eBook) 979-8-218-48515-3

Printed in the United States of America, 2024

"The most merciful thing in the world, I think, is the inability of the human mind to correlate all its contents. We live on a placid island of ignorance in the midst of black seas of infinity, and it was not meant that we should voyage far."

-H.P. Lovecraft, *The Call of Cthulhu*

CONTENTS

THE
LAVENDER
FIELDS

DAY

1

There are no words in the English language that can accurately comprehend what I have witnessed. But I will do what I can. Upon a plane of deep purple, where stocks of "lavender" sway in the gentle breeze, green energy covers the ground, and the sky is filled with an orange haze, and swirling above are particles of purple, dancing around like leaves in autumn caught in a whirlwind. The shrubs on the "flower" pulsate with glitter, like light shining off water. And as I move about from stock to stock...I see life. Deep within the delicate petals of each "plant" reveal a human life, an animal life, an insect, a lizard, a bird, a mammal, a fish. Even plants, trees, flowers, grass. Something as small as an amoeba, a cell, an atom. There are no borders or nations across countries, races, and ethnicities, old and young—a life examined from outsiders' view.

This one, standing tall and full of pride, a young man in Japan strides down the street in the suit his mother bought him for Christmas. He walks to his office job, where he will write his weekly reports, only to return home to his loving wife and children and do it all again the next day. And as I watch his life go by, beside me, another life begins to form. Sprouting out from the ground, the petals begin forming, and the lavender scent hits my nose. This one, newly sprouted, I look within its

I

shrubs, and a baby is being born in America, screaming to return to non-existence. His mother holds him with a glimmer of hope in her eye. Even with her husband gone, off living in Ohio with some bimbo from the slums, she still has hope. Another one, much older, its stem is slumped over. I look within to find an old woman sitting at a nursing home in Germany; her children haven't visited her in months, her husband is long dead, and she's left to wonder when her time has come. And it seems that the time is now. She slumps in her chair, and I watch her take her final breath, and the light leaves her eyes. She is dead. In that same instant, the flower begins to wilt, losing its color and turning grey. It falls apart and disintegrates into a puff of purple. What's left behind is like the petals of a dandelion being blown away, filling the orange sky with dots of lavender.

I watch as the lion in the Sahara pounces on a gazelle, as an owl flies into the headlights of a car in the dead of night, as a little girl flushes her goldfish down the toilet, her tears dripping into the toilet water. I watch as a tree in the Amazon rainforest crashes to the ground, a blade of grass is cut down by a lawnmower, and lavender flowers are plucked from their bundles. I watch as cancer cells grow in a man's brain, the cells struggling to survive, clinging to life, just like the man himself. And I watch as the first atom is split in two, and the explosion rings; the whole world is changed forever.

A continuous cycle of life and death. A baby is born, someone falls in love, the business is successful, a trip to Italy goes according to plan, and someone survives the surgery. So much life but much more death. War, genocide, someone dies of hunger, someone homeless dies from the cold, a newborn baby dies from SIDS, car crashes, cancer, heart attacks, and old age. Some die in their homes, some die in the street, some die filled *with love, most with hate and regret. In my short time here, I have seen it all. All these lives coming to an end, only to find…nothing.*

Some of the lives that I have seen are not for the faint of heart. For they are tales of the strange and unnatural, lives filled with a supernatural presence that no human was meant to discover. For example, I came across a lavender plant bearing the fruit of a young girl and the tragedy that fell before her.

"You must become one with the suffering, with the meaninglessness of the world."

IF MEMORY SERVES ME

We scurry through the darkened woods, our feet crunching on leaves and twigs as we run toward the abandoned church.

"The sisters are waiting, Alice," says Jessica. "The sisters are waiting."

Jessica, my sister, is the only person I have left. Twenty-five years of age, she saw to taking care of me after my mother and father died. I am only 17 now, and I don't turn 18 for another year. My family, the Moores, have been in Rayberg for generations. It's our home, and there was no way we would leave. Especially now.

We come upon the lonesome hill, where the abandoned church stands atop. There used to be a cross that stood tall on the spire, but it was soon taken down. And although abandoned, it was a packed house tonight as it had been every night since the Chambers Sisters came to town.

***

They arrived by bus, of all things. The town of Rayburg, Kansas, is not known for much. If you look us up on the internet, you'll see we have a population of about 1,000 people; you'll find that we have the largest bail of hay, thanks to farmer Jane, and we host the largest Cinnamon Roll festival in all of Kansas. So these two girls turned heads; there was no doubt about that. Clambering out in all-black clothing, the two of them looked no older than 30, with jet-black hair, skinny as rails, and both wearing black dresses. They rented a room at the Rayberg Motel, and Sal let them live there free of charge. Sal Nico, the man who charges you for ice and makes guests wash their own sheets before they leave, or you'll be charged for that too. They quickly set up shop at Annie's Antiques, which, after being open for more than 30 years, Annie Sand gladly sold her storefront to these two newcomers. They changed it from antiques and instead opened up Chambers Coffee Shop in the summertime.

"Weird people, but excellent iced coffees," was the consensus of the townsfolk.

They were always spoken of together and referred to as "the sisters." No one knew their names. They either never mentioned them, or everyone forgot. I can't remember, so they remained "the sisters," becoming one entity in the minds of Raybergians.

The young people quickly took a liking to the coffee shop. The boys were attracted to them, boys will be boys. And the girls were happy to have such independent women around. And that's when their rhetoric began to spread. The young were the first recruited. Abandoning their post of school and family, quickly joining a new family. That of the Chambers. Those who joined were brought into the fold and given employment in the coffee shop. There were no hourly wages, mind you. Instead, all income was given to the sisters and distributed out to the other members. The Chambers took the larger cut. Eventually, they allowed the children to take shelter in the coffee shop itself, setting up cots in the basement. And though it was filled with mold and dust, the children accepted it gladly.

The word CULT began to float around town. Older generations hated them like the "communist bastards" they were, and the parents just wanted their children back. But whenever a parent came rushing in, their hatred quickly turned to admiration, and soon, they would be brought into the fold. After several more parents abandoned their homes to take residence in the coffee shop, the police became involved. Several officers stormed into the place, grabbing children by the arms, punching parents, smashing glasses, and throwing chairs out the window. They wanted the message to be loud and clear: the Chambers Sisters were no longer welcome.

The children were brought into custody, and the coffee shop was in ruins. But the children did not rot in their cells. Just a couple of hours later, their parents rescued the children. Not by the payment of bail but with the bludgeoning of mop handles and the slashing of broken coffee mugs. The parents, under some sort of trance, stormed the police station and "rescued" their kids. The police opened fire, and some parents died, but they managed to overtake them all. My parents were some of the few who died, and my sister was one of the children locked up. They then left the police station and immediately began rebuilding the coffee shop. I remember the Chambers Sisters seemed quite unphased during all of this.

I was left alone in the house, and my sister brought me into the fold. Soon, the entire town was under their thumb. Even Pastor Michaels, who looked at all his altar boys funnily, allowed the sisters to use the abandoned church on the hill in whatever manner they so desired. The church had been under the protection of the town and was deemed a national landmark by the state. The Miracle of Rayberg Church has stood since 1878 and has been held as a place of worship for over 100 years. If you go to City Hall and look through the records, you can find newspaper clippings reporting on its construction. And one of the workers was my great-great-grandfather. Throughout my childhood, my parents would tell me about that small little church, and I would feel a small sense of pride.

But soon, Rayberg developed larger and larger, bringing in more money to build a larger, much nicer church. The Rayberg Halleluhah Cathedral was built in 1989 and has been the designated place of worship ever since. But the Chambers Sisters didn't particularly like the cathedral. They said it "reeked of the hubris of mankind." Or something like that. They instead fell in love with the Miracle of Rayberg and soon began holding congregation, and that's when we were introduced to the rituals. That was 7 years ago.

***

Against the backdrop of a starless sky and the moon working overtime, the church is the brightest thing. A lighthouse, guiding lost sailors to their salvation. My sister and I walk up the hill, our legs getting a little tired from the trek, and we enter the church. The entire town has arrived; some are sitting in pews, and most are standing or sitting on the floor. People squished together like melted marshmallows against mildew wood. The church has been fully restored, painted all white, with mahogany pews and red carpeting. All idols were destroyed. Any semblance of a Christian nation has long since been forgotten.

We take our seat next to Florence Haggerty, 60 years old, who used to scream at the children passing by outside her window. She is sitting beside lil' Johnny Amsley, a 7-year-old who just last week killed a squirrel in a case of strange fascination he could not understand. Johnny is not worried at all sitting next to Officer Chet, 28, who looks at black people the way someone might look at maggots at the bottom of their rotting garbage can, and he does not care sitting next to Terry Gurney, 35, one of said black men, who used to do cocaine outside the back alley of the police station out of spite.

No small town is a stranger to its gossip and dramas, but most folks keep it to themselves and chat about it behind closed doors. But the Chambers Sisters believed in no secrets. After they set themselves up in the City Hall, Mayor Hafford graciously stepped down from his position and gave it to the sisters. They were in charge of everything. Every decision went through them. And as a sign of good faith, they made a point to visit each resident in their home. Dirty laundry was aired, grievances were resolved, and throughout their daily visits to each storefront or the offices of civil servants, they would openly talk about the gossip and drama of Rayberg. With nothing left to hide behind each other's backs, the town felt more at ease with each other. Things were going well. The state of Kansas sent a representative over to check on the new mayors and were pleasantly surprised. One of Kansas's biggest exports is edible cereal, and we ranked #1 out of the rest of the state. Crime was reduced to 0, and we ranked highest in education. Rayburg was prosperous. People wanted to move here, but unfortunately for them, the Chambers sisters were not accepting "new members." The state was okay with that as long as the town was making money. If they bothered to look closer at the numbers, they would've noticed that the population has been decreasing as the years go by. Where did they go? They don't care.

After a few minutes of anticipation, they appear. No one heard the doors open or saw them outside the church beforehand. They simply appeared. Faces covered in black veils to match their black wedding dresses as they walk down the aisle with grace akin to floating, never looking toward the pews to meet eyes glistening with admiration. They walk up the steps to the stage and slowly turn to meet us. The mass begins.

"Welcome, everyone. The Forgotten smile upon you this night, and the Remembered tremble before your might. Tonight, another of you shall be initiated. To become one with the cosmos and live with eternity. Who shall it be?" said the sisters in unison.

The silence hangs in the air. The selection process is based on performance, how hard you worked in the town, and how impactful your service is to the community. Every three months, the sisters compile the data, logged-in hours, community service, earned income, social changes, and word of mouth. They maintain it all and make a decision based on their findings. Marion Finch, the local baker who slept with every farmer this side of Kansas, sits up from her seat and quickly walks toward the stage. She's holding an envelope, which, when opened, will reveal the chosen who shall ascend. Marion hands them the envelope, looking up at the Chamber Sisters with awe. The sisters do not move; only one extends their hand out to grab the envelope. Their never-blinking eyes stare out amongst the crowd, and their non-existent smile is hidden behind their blackened veils. Marion fades to a look of distress, and she rushes back to sit next to Brittany Jarvis, the 17-year-old girl who aspires to be a doctor and has been studying the effects of rat poison in her brother's food.

They open the envelope.

"Nathan Alexander!" they shout in unison.

"Praise be!" sobs Nathan.

Nathan Alexander, a 30-year-old man, is crying like a baby. He kneels in his pew upon the cushioned rest placed underneath the pew in front, clasping his hands in gratitude. Tears and snot trickle and traverse through his knuckles and the lines in his palms. He was clasping so hard that his face turned red, and his veins popped out of his arms. I thought he was going to start bleeding from the eyes. Nathan Alexander works as a veterinarian at Alert for Animals, the smallest veterinarian office in the county. He is polite, he is punctual, and most importantly, he loves animals. However, he suffered from Bipolar disorder and was prone to bouts of depression, which would lead to bouts of anger. So there would be times when pets would go missing when pets were found drowned in the rivers or mutilated in their owner's backyards. And there was Nathan, to console the grieving and to clean up the mess. Always smiling. But that soon stopped once the sisters came into town. Everyone's filthy habits seemed to stop. During the sister's visits to resident homes, grievances between townsfolk would be solved, illnesses cured, and demons cast out. Like I said, they brought a calmness with them.

Murmurings in the crowd begin. They are not sighs of relief but harumphs of anger. They had all put in their hours, lost sleep, and drained their blood, sweat, and tears into this town, only to wait another 3 months. Some are excited. Nathan's wife and children are hugging him and congratulating him over his sobs. His wife is crying along with him. The Chambers sisters come down from the stage and slowly make their way to the exit. Nathan's wife sees this and pats her husband on the back to get off the knee rest. The sisters exit the church, Nathan and his family follow suit, and soon, all of us exit the church in a single file line, just like in school.

We all stand around the large burr oak tree. The sisters light candles in a circle and add sigils to the tree. The tree is covered in these sigils made up of names from rituals past. Dozens of sigils around the tree, each representing a previous member of this community, all of which we have forgotten. *That* was the miracle the Chambers Sisters provided, to be forgotten. When they first took over Rayburg, I mentioned they visited every resident in town. They spoke to the residents, and the residents voiced their wants, needs, and concerns. And at the end of it all, the Chambers Sisters would sit them down, and they would be shown. Shown the true nature of things.

A flying deity mashed with feathered wings and bulbous foreheads, eyes all over, and a massive field of lilies surrounding its gelatinous form of fat and cellulite that hung over its eyes, limiting its sight. This is God. Or at least the God of the Chambers Sisters. They called it Oblivio, Latin for forgetfulness. They told stories of the deity forgetting its own existence. It forgot its name, its purpose, its origins, but because of this, it was happy. Day in and day out, it would forget each day, not remembering the last, and could begin anew. This being was like a child, everything new, everything exciting, never knowing the horrors of the world and the suffering of the universe. The Chambers Sisters worshiped this deity, believing non-existence to be better than existence and that being forgotten is the only moral act. Not to die, but to not exist. Not to simply be forgotten by friends and family, but to never be known at all. The universe itself never knew you were a cog in its ever-mighty machine.

The Chambers Sisters explained that they had been around a long time, their life span expanded by the ignorance of Oblivio. They made contact with him thousands of years ago and discovered that Oblivio had been able to reclaim his memories through the devouring of other individuals. Oblivio is God, the oldest God, the only God, the God where all else stems from; he just doesn't know it. Repressed memories bubbling to the surface only by the absorption of other people. Their memories, their soul, their life force. And so, a deal was struck. With each passing person sacrificed to the forgetful God, the Chambers Sisters were granted everlasting life. So they traveled and spread the good word. Who knows how many people, how many towns, cities, states, countries, and continents, what lost civilizations or lost hikers, and how many future settlements and broken caravans were erased because of the Sisters and their God. Who knows how many of our fellow townsfolk, community members, neighbors, friends, and family have been wiped from our memories? No one remembers. And I suppose that's the point. What luck had become upon them that they were chosen to become a child of Oblivio. I lose sleep sometimes thinking about it. And the fact that a pompous, animal-snuffing ass like Nathan Alexander should be chosen makes my blood boil and my heart break.

The sisters are waiting. Nathan Alexander can sense their impatience and walks toward them, toward the great tree. He stands in the circle of candles, and in the center are ancient symbols unrecognizable to any culture or religion. Nathan calmed down from a few moments ago, and he's all smiles now. He looks back to his wife and children, and they couldn't be more proud. His wife is still crying, and the children look at their father as if he were about to achieve sainthood. Which he is.

"Nathan Alexander, you have been deemed worthy by Oblivio, to join him in his ranks, to bolster his power, and to ever be forgotten in a cruel, cruel universe. Do you have anything to say before you ascend?" declared the sisters.

Nathan turns to us with expressions of delight and gratitude. He addresses us all loud and clear as he makes his final declaration of this world.

"I just want to say that I am honored to be chosen for something as…as *big* as this. I used to be a God-fearing man, but that was before Oblivio. Even back then, it just didn't feel right. There was so much believing in nothing; I always felt like I was praying to the wind, praying on deaf ears. But then these beautiful, angelic women showed up in our lives and changed everything. I can't thank them enough, and I can't thank you all enough. We've been a community for so long; you all are just like family. I mean, don't get me wrong, some of you were pushing my last nerve. Some of you, I just wanted to upright KILL!" Nathan screams, laughing.

A nervous laugh trickles through the crowd.

"But that all changed with Oblivio and the dedication and structure he gives to our lives. My family's lives. Donna, Mary Beth, and my big boy Ricky. You mean the world to me, and I love you all so much. I hope you can look at me and be proud of the man that I have become. Of the service that I have provided for this town and of the sacrifice I am making. Thank you."

The crowd begins to applaud. I'm trying hard not to vomit in my mouth. But I'm keeping composure.

"Then, if all is said, let us commence the ascension," said the sisters.

The flames of the candles rise as they lift their hands into the air. And then the chanting begins:

"Utinam te in arma oblivio tollas ac deleas. Sit tam longa quies quam clarissimus ortu solis tranquillus. Et numquam te mundus pertulit in orbem."

(May Oblivio take you into their arms and erase you from existence. May the long sleep be as peaceful as the brightest sunrise. And may the universe never bore you back into the world.)

The crowd chants in unison; the sisters lead the chant and repeat the phrase over and over and over. And now that Nathan Alexander has risen 4 feet off the ground and gradually rising, he now appears to me clearer than ever. He's nothing but a speck, an insignificant dust bunny off to some Neverland that we will all be joining. But not soon enough. I am jealous. Envious. My sister and I work harder than anyone else in town. My sister especially. Everyone *loves* her. The poor beautiful girl takes care of her sister all by herself, works a full-time job, and still finds time to worship Oblivio to the fullest. And I'm just…there. The lonesome girl who can barely fend for herself, who crashed into the mailbox learning to drive, who can't cook grilled cheese without burning it, who can't make friends with the other girls, and who regularly forgets to leave her weekly offering to Oblivio. Things like my favorite books, favorite foods, or favorite clothes, an exercise in forgetfulness. But how could I forget my mother's favorite sweater, my father's favorite watch, or the books Jessica used to read every night? Memories of better times, memories of the ones I love. All to be forgotten.

Nathan rises higher and higher. 7 feet, 10 feet, 20 feet, 40 feet, 200 feet, higher and higher and higher. Past the church, past the tallest trees, climbing higher than the moon and the stars, past the Milky Way galaxy, across the farthest universes, until a radiant blast of light twinkles across the night sky, like an exploding meteor or dying star. His dumb-witted smile fades farther from sight until it's nothing less than a speck. His voice drifts off farther and farther; his cries to his family, his begging for forgiveness, and his pleas of joy are nothing more than silent muffles and empty echoes. Only Oblivio can hear him now, and I'm sure he'll forget.

We chant and watch until they are gone from sight—until the person we once knew is no more of this world. The chanting lulls its chanters into a trance and empties our thoughts. As we chant, our memories of the person are slowly erased from our minds, and once they are gone from sight, the knowledge of their existence is as barren as the desert. I cannot tell you who was chosen, who they were, or what they did. They simply do not exist.

"And so the ritual is complete. Another child is off to join Oblivio into the nothingness. Go now, and pray that you will be next in his sights, " the sisters said to the crowd.

With that, the crowd dispersed. Heading off toward the woods, back to Rayberg, back to their homes, to pray to Oblivio. Jessica grabs my hand and leads me back home. I look over to Donna Alexander and her children. The woman has tears in her eyes but does not look upset. As if she had been crying before, but she doesn't remember why. She holds her children close, giving them hugs and kisses. Like she had lost something she cannot remember, and is holding on to what she knows. Holding on for dear life.

***

At Rayberg High School, in an English class with 20 kids, including myself, one stands in front of all as the child who got the highest grade on the final exam. Sally Sue studied hard for the exam on MacBeth, which we had spent all of the last semester reading in class. Her parents, wanting the best for their daughter, and holding hope that Oblivio would choose her, pushed her hard and forced her to study every night. Long, tearful hours spent pouring over those monologues and soliloquies.

"The weird sisters, hand in hand,
Posters of the sea and land,
Thus do go about, about."
-Macbeth, 1.3

And there she stands, proud and tall. Her hands are behind her back, a large smile across her face. As for the other children, they looked distraught, to say the least. Marv Hamilton is shaking with fear, sweat dripping down his face. Harriet Neeves is grabbing the edges of her desk with anger, about to pull the wood off of the metal frame. And Yvette Anderson is crying in the corner, snot dripping out of her nose, and a small puddle of pee forming around her feet. Mrs. Hubman is sitting at her desk, looking across the room with a sense of achievement. Surely, she has gained Oblivio's favor, for she has done her job well in spotlighting the highest-marked student in the class and "motivating" the children to do better next time. It also helps that she fudged the numbers a bit.

Mrs. Hubman had been under hot water before the Chambers Sisters arrived. One day, while the children were at the library having computer time, a large amount of pornography was discovered on the school's shared hard drive. Us children had a field day with that. The police were involved, and through thorough investigation by Officer Gustav, who had a real taste for these types of genres, was able to determine that these specific porn videos had been released in the last couple of months, so whoever it was, had used the computer very recently. The school carefully searched through all of the security tapes, looking at each individual who used the school computers and looking at repeat offenders. They narrowed it down to a few suspects: Ted Farady, the janitor, who wraps himself in tinfoil every night and awaits his weekly visit from the aliens; Janice Yung, the guidance counselor, who has a voodoo doll of every student handmade under her desk, and then there was Alice Hubman, who definitely was the one watching pornography at the school. They did never officially charge her for anything, but we all knew. During the Chambers Sister's visits, Alice admitted to being a sex addict, so everyone assumed it was her. She needed to get back in the school's good graces. She was due for a raise, and if she had outperformed her peers, she would be able to make tenure and be nominated for a Kansas Teacher of the Year Award. That would most definitely put her in Oblivio's favor. So she fudged the numbers, gave Sally Sue better grades than she actually had, and maybe even gave some other students some bad grades. Why Sally Sue? She looked at the class sheet, closed her eyes, and randomly picked a name. Sally Sue was the lucky girl who got to have the best grades in the class and get a full scholarship to the University of Kansas.

Competition. That was the currency in Rayburg. The town became a cesspool of envy. Every move you made, every hand you waved, every smile, every greeting, every customer assistance, lending of a hand, favor to be asked, service to your community, food prepared, dollars earned, bill paid, was all in the service of Oblivio. They didn't even really care about money. Keeping just enough to support themselves, and all the rest going to the sisters. Everyone wanted to be in his good graces. Some thought prayer would get them there, and others thought the sisters were the way to Oblivio's heart. People donated lots of money to them, donated their belongings and their time. Becoming their servants and doing errands and chores for them. Some worked long hours at the coffee shop for little to no pay. One of those people is my sister Jessica. She dedicates herself to that place; she bends over backward to prepare coffee for the citizens of Rayberg. With their fake smiles, polite gestures, hardy handshakes, and dad jokes. Jessica smiles through it and replies in kindness. She is a star employee. Memorizing people's orders and having every recipe down to a science. But she's not perfect. Now and again, she slips up. Too much cream, not enough milk, that's not what they ordered. And she smiles through it. But some days, when I come to visit her on her break, I find her in the back of the shop. Crying in the fetal position, banging her fists against her head, calling herself stupid, stupid, stupid, over and over and over. Only stopping when I reach for her hands.

But even I must admit Oblivio's hold on me. That night on the last ritual, I do not remember the person or my relation to them, but I could feel the anger. The anger of not being chosen. In reality, I was at the top of my class. I study the hardest out of all of my peers, I read the books on the syllabus months before they are assigned, and I finish all of my homework within the hour. Call me stupid for wanting to learn. So when I saw that my grades were slipping and little Miss Sally Sue was doing better than me, I knew something was wrong. Sally Sue, the girl who used to shove crayons up her nose until last year. One night, I broke into the school and I went into Mrs. Hubmans office. I checked her files and saw what she was doing. She was giving Sally Sue the highest marks, and slightly lowering the rest of the class's grades. But mine, specifically, were going down the most. On all of my papers, she was marking more of my answers wrong when they were right. And on all of my papers, in red marker, in big bold letters, she wrote: TEACHERS PET.

You see, in the doctrine of Oblivio, through the words of the Chambers Sisters, kindness is a sin. Kindness is what leads to hatred. We only suffer in the world because of a lack of happiness. You wouldn't know that evil is bad if you haven't experienced good. So to become one with Oblivio, one must eradicate happiness. You must become one with the suffering, with the meaninglessness of the world. Only then will you truly know and appreciate what it means to not exist. To be forgotten.

The next ritual is not for a couple of months. It's the only thing I have to look forward to, the only thing that is keeping me going. I guess if there's one thing I can relate to those religious types, it's the act of faith. The hope that I have, that I might be chosen, that I might be wiped from this wretched existence, that I might be forgotten by my sister, never having to worry about me. That I might forget about my parents and the pain of their loss. That I might forget about my classmates, that I might forget about Rayberg, that I might forget about life itself. Just the very thought, warms my heart and calms me to sleep.

***

Jessica and I arrive at the church. Normally, we try to sit as close to the front as possible, but we arrived a little later; it was full. So we just sit in the back beside Renald Kurt, who thinks the FBI is spying on him with a camera in his toothpaste tube. It's been over a year. The church has decayed so much; the wood has splintered, the paint has decayed, and the red carpet has turned a soft brown. As well as the church being worn down, the Raybergians have been feeling the same. They never stop. Every day, they work till the sun rises, 12-hour days in the office, at the construction site, or at the coffee shop. And any time not working is spent in prayer. Jessica has especially been working overtime, dedicating herself completely. But Oblivio is a hard God to please, and it never feels like enough. She just became employee of the month at the coffee shop, and the sisters personally gave her a statue of Oblivio as a token of their gratitude in recognition of her service to the cause. Oh, how the great Raybergians gritted their teeth in fake smiles and clenched fists on that day. But no matter how many hours she puts in, no matter how much she tries to please the sisters, no matter how much she prays, no matter how much she meditates on non-existence, no matter how much of her food she sacrifices to the great forgetful one; it's never enough. She's not eating, she's bone thin, bags under her eyes and her hair is greasy. She's not showering, she barely leaves the house, and all her time is spent on holy matters. Without my money from the waitressing job I got, I think my sister would go completely over the edge. And I'm clinging on for dear life myself. The wonderful management at Mikey's Tavern has promoted me to bartender, even though I am underage. This means instead of old men groping me; I now have old men threatening to murder me because I don't make their Jack and Coke exactly how they like it. And with how Mrs. Hubman handled my grades, I couldn't get into Kansas University and instead had to settle for Rayberg Community College. I'm stretching myself thin. I tried to tell the Sisters about Mrs. Hubman, but they wouldn't listen.

They've been strange lately. Stranger than usual. The townsfolk noticed it too. They were beginning to look...different. Older. They recently relocated to the center of town at the Howard Mansion, owned by the famous philanthropist Howard Phillips before he died of rabies in 1887. And per their orders, citizens were allowed to visit them with any questions or concerns they may have. This was going on fairly smoothly, with people having questions about how to appease Oblivio, asking about their performance in the town, inquiring about the nature of non-existence, and things of that nature. But then, the townsfolk began coming to the mansion with complaints. Bernadette Melanson, for example, had complaints about her current position at the Rayberg Law Firm. She had represented Turner Gentry, a 40-year-old resident, who was driving back from Kansas City after a night of gambling and drinking at the casinos when he drove head-on into the car of Abby Flannigan, a 25-year-old heading back home to Kansas City from a 2-month long road trip. She died instantly. Turner Gentry was hanging on for dear life and unfortunately survived. Bernadette was his defense attorney and represented him well. She was able to convince the jury that even though Turner was under the influence, it was clear that a 25-year-old driving an old beat-down van was more dangerous on the road than he was. And that it was more likely that she crashed into him instead of the other way around. Bernadette won the case, and Turner got away scot-free. So why was she upset with the sisters? Because the prosecutor on the case was chosen to receive the blessings of Oblivio. None of us remember who this prosecutor was, but Bernadette just knew that this person had been chosen over her. She said she could see a faceless person. She could not recall who they were, but in the recesses of her mind, they left an imprint of the relationship they had with one another. She knew that whoever this prosecutor was, they knew each other. And they had been chosen instead of them.

Other townsfolk started reporting similar things. Vague memories of members past, faceless people with only fleeting recollections of their relationships with one another. People who had been chosen over them and demanded to know why. Something that has gone unspoken since this all started is the strange effect that the Chambers Sisters have on the population of Rayberg. Ever since they arrived, they seem to get whatever they want and face no resistance from anyone. As though they had cast some sort of spell over the town, one that forces people to adhere to their charm, to make them admit to all of their secrets and dirty laundry, and to cater to their every will. But over time, it seems as though that spell has been fading. As I mentioned, they've been looking older. They told us that the sacrifices of our citizens are what give them their youth and immortality. But over the past year, even with a regular amount of sacrifices, they seem to be losing their power, and their magic is fading. Oblivio is the God of forgetfulness, and maybe he has simply forgotten the Chambers Sisters. What once they were a source of sustenance for him, maybe he has simply forgotten sustenance itself. A God of non-existence would not need such things. Perhaps the sisters were too confident in their dealings. For although they gave a great gift to Oblivio, they did not take into account that a God needs no gifts. That non-existence requires nothing. But still, the sisters carried on the rituals, hoping that their God had not abandoned them. Or us. Or me.

The service plays out the same as it has all these years. The sisters appear from the ether, entering the church with their black wedding dresses, veils covering their now wrinkled faces, and black gloves to cover the blotches and veins on their hands. They're not as strong as they used to be, so they appointed Jenny and Damien Filtch, a married couple who pray to Oblivio to forget about their dead son, who they miss and love throughout their days, to accompany them onto the stage. They hold the sister's arms as they guide them up to the podium. The sisters grab their bearings, and then the Filtchs scramble to take their seats.

"Welcome, our friends. I am so glad that we can gather again to praise Oblivio and rejoice in non-existence. Now, let us see who will be the chosen one today," said the sisters in unison.

Marion Finch, who has still not been chosen, rises from her seat and quickly hands over an envelope before rushing back to her seat. She doesn't even meet the sisters' eyes. Their power is not as it once was, but their fear is ever present. They open the envelope.

"Jessica Moore," said the sisters.

The name hangs in the silence. The crowd turns around, looking to the back of the church, to meet the eyes of Jessica and me. Her mouth is agape, her legs shake, her eyes wide, and tears stream down her face. A smile begins to form as she stands up to gaze upon the crowd. And there I am, looking up to her, like the mad Titans looking up to Olympus.

***

"Utinam te in arma oblivio tollas ac deleas. Sit tam longa quies quam clarissimus ortu solis tranquillus. Et numquam te mundus pertulit in orbem."

The crowd begins their chant as the sisters add Jessica's sigil to the tree. She begins to rise, higher and higher above the crowd, circling the candles and ancient symbols. She's waving at me from above, and I can't manage to do anything. I stand as still as a statue, looking up at her with all the rage I can muster. It doesn't need to be said. That should be me up there. I was the true prodigal son of the town. She might have been the rising star, but I was the hidden prophet waiting in the wings. Everyone loved Jessica; her undying devotion to the cause made her the obvious choice. But I am the true chosen. I truly understand non-existence. To never want to be alive and to have your existence erased. My sister hasn't been out in the world, she hasn't had opportunities taken away from her, and she doesn't know what people are like. The poor and destitute at Mikey's Tavern, the weary travelers, recovering prostitutes, struggling alcoholics, and lonely souls, they told me their stories. Divorces, child abuse, domestic assault, police brutality, hunger, homelessness, loved ones lost, dreams crushed, hearts broken, and the flame of life extinguished. The world outside of Rayberg looked a lot bleaker than she or a lot of the other citizens realize. But I realize. I realize the reason why Oblivio is a forgetful God and why he chooses non-existence over life. Because the world is horrifying. And to remember any of it is worse than any death or cosmic punishment. It is simply better to have not existed at all. I understand this. And yet I am down here, and Jessica is up there.

I watch as she rises, higher and higher and higher. 20 feet, 100 feet, 500 feet, 1200 feet. I can't stand to look at her anymore. That stupid smile on her face, the crowd chanting, the old sisters barely holding on. I'm done. It's over. I look to the ground and find a large rock. I hold myself high, take aim, and let loose like a catapult. It flies through the air, and for a moment, time stands still. I look at my sister, and I remember. I remember us playing softball in the backyard, riding our bikes through the neighborhood, and staying up late to watch movies. I remember her walking me to school and sticking up for me when bullies crawled out of the woodwork. I remember her holding me as I cried when Patty Kent tricked me into thinking that Fernando Jenkins wanted to kiss me in the girl's bathroom, and instead, she and a group of girls were waiting to dump toilet water all over me. I remember when Jessica cut school, came over to the middle school, and in the middle of class, dumped toilet water all over Patty. She was lucky she got suspended and not expelled. But she took that risk for me. Before all of this happened, we just loved each other. Purely and instinctly. We're sisters, bonded by blood, to stand by each other through thick and thin. But in an instant, in a flash of rage, all of that is gone. All of what our sisterhood stood for had vanished, and all of our love was crushed beneath rock and stone.

The rock made its impact. Smashing Jessica on the side of the head, the blood falling like rain and splattering across the crowd. Her head whips back in mid-air, and the chanting begins to fade. The silence is heavy as my sister falls like a rag doll, crashing down on scared ground. I look on in horror as I inch closer to Jessica. The crowd parts way for me, allowing me to enter into the center of the circle of candles, where my sister lay dead by my hand. I kneel and grab her body. The pain hasn't hit me yet, and I don't know if it will. A part of me wants to scream out in pain, to scream in agony at the sight of my handiwork. But another part of me is happy, hoping that Oblivio will forgive me for taking this gift away from him, and to allow me to go in my sister's place. I hold her lifeless body in my arms; the lights have left her eyes, her lips are turning blue, and her skin is pale white. The blood is all over my hands. The Chambers sisters enter the center of the circle.

"Alice Moore, you will be remembered. Your name will ring throughout the cosmos. Your essence will permeate like a stain throughout history. The Earth will reject you, and the worms and the dirt will pass over your body, and you will never return home to whence you came. Your family name will be dragged through the mud, and they will never find retribution. You will never feel the sweet embrace of Oblivio and the gift he provides us. Non-existence will never reach your soul. You will be remembered. This day, and every day, till there are no more days," the sisters declared.

The Chambers Sisters, no longer needing the help of the Filtches, walk off into the dark wilderness. The crowd begins to disperse. One at a time, the townsfolk go their separate ways, back to their homes, back to their lives. And I am there alone, Jessica still in my arms. The tears begin to stream like a broken dam.

DAY
7

Who am I again? I can't forget. My name is… I don't remember! What do I remember? I'm a NASA scientist, I joined in the year 4047, and I took flight on The Elysian in 4057 to observe a unique phenomenon. Two asteroids were going to collide in front of Sagittarius A, a black hole in the center of the Milky Way Galaxy. A once-in-a-lifetime opportunity, and we were to observe the after-effects and report back our findings. But when the two asteroids collided in a beautiful explosion, it created a tear in space-time. We were too close to the black hole, and when this explosion happened, it disabled all the ship's functions, including our gravitational "anchor," locking us in place so Sagittarius A didn't suck us in. But now, it was pulling us in the direction of the tear. Our ship passed through, and we were transported to somewhere outside of space-time.

A tear is very different from a wormhole, which allows you to travel through space-time, creating a shortcut from one fixed point in space-time to another. The classic example is taking a sheet of paper, putting two dots on each end, folding the paper so the two points meet, and putting a pencil through the two holes: a wormhole. But what if, when traveling between the dots, instead of going straight through the wormhole, you went outside it? A wormhole is a tear, but it's a fixed tear. If you travel outside the two points, you end up in the "inbetween."

When traveling through a wormhole, you can travel anywhere in space-time, but only within your own space-time. Einstein said we are all insects trapped in a soap bubble, and naturally, he assumed there would be other soap bubbles out there. A multiverse. An infinite amount of universes, each with its own variations. All possible worlds, all possible existing realities.

A world where Hitler never rose to power, we never split the atom, Jesus never gave his sermon on the mount, Pompeii never erupted, Amelia Earheart finished her journey, green means stop and red means go, a world where you had eggs instead of toast for breakfast, a world where we are comprised of arsenic instead of carbon, a world where we never leaped consciousness, we remained in our neanderthal state, and instead of us, it was dogs that gained our destined intelligence. Dog coffee shops with pup cups and kibble, dog historians that study the ancient wolf ancestor and their societies, dog business meetings that begin with the sniffing of behinds instead of handshakes, and dog funerals that end with howls in the sky. The human is reduced to nothing more than a pet, domesticated and subjugated. Human vets, human parks, and human shows with different human breeds. Humans will have to be fixed, have their bellies scratched, have their noses rubbed in shit, and some will be put in human fighting matches for all to see. I've seen it all. All possible worlds, all possible existing realities. And each of these soap bubbles lives in a different dimension.

Each of these soap bubbles lives in a different dimension, with each dimension stacked on top of one another. There are 10 dimensions. We experience the first four every day: Length, Width, Depth, and Time. The fifth through the tenth all have to do with multiple universes. Each dimension gains more and more of the possibility of different universes, each with different start conditions, some with the same, and all of the different branches that result from these. And the tenth dimension is where we would see everything and learn everything. Every possible variation, every possible timeline, every possible history, every version of everyone, including every version of you. We would see and know all at once. This is the lavender fields. Time is irrelevant here. What felt like days and weeks and years all at once was only a matter of seconds. We passed the dimensional layers, entering into higher dimensions, witnessing stranger and stranger universes until we reached the highest level possible.

I woke up alone, with no sign of my crew. My helmet broke, but the air was breathable; the gravity was like that of Earth. I've been wandering for a week and haven't felt the need to eat or drink. I took off my suit and found my journal in my pocket. I could feel myself slipping away. All these different universes, all these worlds, all these lives, they're all starting to blend with my own life. I have to write it down. Everything. Everything that I've seen, and heard, and felt. I'll write it all down. I can't forget.

"For the first time in his dull life, Lucky was excited to be alive."

TIME WILL TELL

Lucky had never been lucky. On the day of his birth, Lucky had his mother's umbilical cord wrapped around his neck twice. The doctors had to perform an emergency C-section to stop him from choking. It's a miracle he made it out alive. He was Lucky. Weighing at 5 pounds, 3 ounces, Lucky had his whole life ahead of him. But from that day on, it had seemed like a cruel joke from God that nothing ever went his way. Every test he ever took, he failed. Even though he swears he studied, which he didn't. Every girl he ever talked to, told him he was creepy, which he was. Every boss that ever fired him told him he was a lazy bastard, which he was. And both his parents told him he would never amount to anything, which he wouldn't.

Lucky had no ambition. He had no desire to learn or to improve. He couldn't do math; he didn't know history; he couldn't read or write past a 9th-grade level; he couldn't play guitar; he couldn't sing, he couldn't dance, or work a cash register, sweep the floors, stock the shelves, or cut the meat. He couldn't drive or ride a bike, he couldn't throw a baseball or a football, he couldn't kick a soccer ball, and he missed the golf ball with his club every time. And no matter how much his teachers encouraged him, no matter how much his boss yelled at him, and no matter how many late-night talks of disappointment his parents had with him, Lucky would not change. And it wasn't his upbringing. Lucky's father had been a firefighter, a hero to the local community. His mother had been a school teacher, fostering the future generation. His parents were successful, upstanding members of society. The apple falls far from the tree, as the saying goes.

But one day, on his 40th birthday, Lucky began to feel sad. He sat in his apartment in New York City, a small wooden room containing a bed, with the toilet and sink in the same room. The room was so small that he had to keep all of his clothes in a trunk under his bed, as well as all of his other belongings, which consisted of a pocket watch his grandfather gave him and a sack full of quarters for future use. He was sitting on his tiny bed with one blanket, no bedsheets, and a feather pillow. He thought back to every instance of bad luck and realized that maybe he could've done better. He could've studied better, he could've been nicer, he could've tried harder at work or his hobbies. He could've listened to his parents, his teachers, and his mentors. He could've tried harder in relationships, and maybe the one who got away wouldn't have gone away. He was alone. Nobody called him to wish him a happy birthday, no gifts, no cake, no party. No one. And it was in this moment of self-loathing that he got the idea that it might be time to end this wretched existence.

Lucky was a heroin addict. He had picked it up after high school. His coworker at the gas station had offered it to Lucky when he got evicted from his apartment.

"First ones on me," they offered.

The first time Lucky injected the black tar into his veins, he knew love for the very first time. A love that never goes away. A warm, short-lived feeling. A euphoric sensation that leaves you wanting more. Utter bliss in a syringe, making you relaxed. You just want to lay there in an ocean of feelings. It's truly enchanting. The taste alone will make you dependent on it, captivating you. It becomes your medicine for the health that is your human condition. An escape from the horrors of the world and the monotony of life. Lucky was spending $50 a day on heroin, even though he was living on unemployment checks, going without food, and begging on the street. He looked no different from the other bums on the street, with his crew cut, stubbly face and skinny frame. A long, slow slide to becoming a cockroach, scrounging on the leftovers of others. Often, he would lie awake at night, asking himself, "Why haven't I died? Why hasn't it taken me out?" When he hadn't used it in a while, he would sweat and have painful cramps, vomiting, and diarrhea. But once he got his fix, all the pain went away. It consumed his life. Spending his days in his coworker's parked van on the side of the road, blankets covering the windows, and riding the waves. He felt ugly, he felt thin, and he felt worthless. Every day, every hit, he didn't know if this was the one that was going to kill him.

He pulled the trunk out from under his bed and found the dirt-stained jeans he wore every day. He needed a hit now; he couldn't wait, and he knew he would often forget a few pouches of heroin here or there in his pants. He rummaged through his pockets, sifting through loose cigarettes and lint, and grabbed onto the small ziplock bag of heroin. He remembers this bag. He bought it from his coworker, and they had warned him that this was some new stuff hitting the streets. Each bag was labeled with a red stamped image of a clock.

"This shit LITERALLY stops time!" they warned him.

Lucky didn't know what that meant. But as long as he was high, he didn't care. He stripped off his clothes; he felt more comfortable in the nude. He sat on his toilet, covered in hair and piss, filled the needle with a lethal dose, and began the process. He was using a large rubber band to isolate the vein, irritating it by flicking it and then injecting the needle into the vein. Pushing that black substance into his body, waiting for the warmth to fill his soul and to feel loved for the last time.

Hours pass. Lucky waited for his body to shut down and for his vision to fade until it was nothing but eternal darkness. But it never arrived. He figured it failed, just like the last time he tried. Several months back, he overdosed, and the medics pumped him with NARCAN. He wasn't trying to die, but he sure didn't fight it when it was happening. He felt his lips go cold, his mind go empty, and the warmth was the strongest it had ever been. He thought about that moment, waiting on his toilet, and it filled him with a weird sense of nostalgia.

Hours and hours, and the warmth continued, never subsiding. Lucky figured if he hadn't died, he wouldn't die anytime soon. It was his birthday, after all, and maybe he could try and make the most of it on his own. He got off his toilet, got dressed, and headed back out into the world.

Exiting his apartment, he passed old lady Kurathers in the stairwell. She is holding a bag of groceries in her apartment, rummaging through her purse for her keys, her left foot on the bottom step, while her right extends to reach the top step. Lucky passed by her, greeting her as he did so, only to turn back around at her silence. Normally, she tells him to "pound sand" or "buzz off". He turned around to find her completely frozen in place. Time stands still as she is trapped in perpetual motion, never putting her tapioca pudding and soy milk into the fridge. He attempted to grab her and move her around, to shake her out of her comatose state, but she would not budge. He tried slapping her, fearing that she might be having some kind of episode. Every slap moved her face in the appropriate direction, leaving red marks across her face and old skin flailing about. And yet, she remained still. There was no physical reaction coming from her, she was everything that she was before this time anomaly occurred, preserved in time for all to see.

Outside of his apartment, he found more of the same. On the streets of New York, crowds upon crowds of people stood like statues in a concrete jungle. A Wall Street businessman takes a sip of his coffee as he strides across the crosswalk, his tie flapping in the wind. A woman is yelling into her cellphone as she pushes a stroller down the sidewalk. A street performer is frozen in the air as he is doing a backflip. A biker zips by pedestrians, only to hit a pothole, and now he is stuck in the air and will never make impact with the concrete. A busker will never get to finish their solo, the taxis will never reach their destination, and the hot dog vendor will never finish squirting ketchup onto the hotdog. Birds trapped mid-light, squirrels mid-climb in trees, and a mosquito mid-suck in a person's arm. The sun sits high in the sky, and it will never set. The moon will never show its shining face, and darkness will retire to a passing memory. Lucky walked amongst the crowds, passing by each time-displaced face. People, with lives of their own, all stopped to a grinding halt on the day of his birth. He could not ignore the significance.

Lucky didn't know what to do. His first thought was that he had indeed died, and this was hell. A world where you can do whatever you want, but no one to enjoy it with. But he figured it's better than being tortured for eternity, so maybe it's more like a purgatory. God would decide what to do with him when he was ready. And while he was waiting, why not have some fun? He'd lived in New York City for almost 10 years, and he never saw the sights. "I'll get to it eventually," he told himself. This was eventually. And hey, it was his birthday today. Why not treat himself? He couldn't catch a train, so he just walked.

He started with Times Square, and it was the first time in a long while that he couldn't take his eyes away from the sky. Long spiraling towers filled his vision, each glaring with different advertisements, bright colors, and lights of different fast food chains, banks, movie posters, broadway musicals, the newest phone, or whatever shit they're trying to shovel down our throats. Lucky could barely see the sky and was entranced by the pretty pictures. Next to the apocryphal billboards are the skyscrapers that reach the seat of God. Each building has thousands of windows, with thousands of people in each one. Each with hopes and dreams, pains and sorrows.

He walked up red stairs; he thought if he walked up to the top, he would make it to the windows. He did not. He looked down over the scores of people. One man was stuck in mid-sneeze, one woman was in mid-cough, a skateboarder in mid-kick-flip, a costumed performer dressed as Winnie the Pooh was mid-dance in front of a crying child, a homeless person in mid-puff of a cigarette, and a businesswoman is mid-bite of a street taco. Lucky saw the fragility, the grossness, and the horror of humanity. Like a painting, all laid out before him. He imagined this is how God saw people, looking down above them, witnessing them in their sin and their filth, wondering why they could not be better.

Lucky made his way to Central Park. He found a nice park bench by the lake and sat next to an old man who was feeding the ducks pieces of bread. The bread hung in the air, never to reach the water or the ducks. He looked out across the lake, admiring how it reflected the sky and the clouds. It was almost as if the lake was a portal to the sky, and if Lucky jumped into the lake, he would not be crashing into the water but falling through the air. To land on a soft, fluffy cloud, like he used to see in cartoons. But he didn't bring a change of clothes, so he decided not to try it.

Then, he made his way to the Bronx Zoo. The lions were hiding in their huts, so he jumped into the pit so he could pet them. Lucky always wanted to pet a lion; their manes looked very soft. And he chuckled, as he thought what a predicament it would be if time were to start back up at this moment. Thankfully, it did not. At the ape enclosure, the chimps were high up in their artificial trees, swinging on tire swings, leaping from branches in a single bound, eating bananas, picking fleas, scratching bums, sniffing fingers, and howling to the sky. Lucky looked at one of the chimps in particular and saw an uncanny resemblance. It looked exactly like him, everything down to the hairs on his chin, to his rounded face, and his dumbfounded expression. Lucky remembered hearing something a long time ago about how humans are related to chimps. But he didn't understand it fully. He tried to look it up on his phone, but his screen was frozen on the video he was watching of a guy punching a kangaroo. He decided to go to the New York Public Library and look it up.

Lucky marvels at the marble pillars, tall archways, and holy men and women etched above. Lucky can't help but be a little freaked out by the lions glaring at him like Cerebus guarding the Underworld. People are entering and exiting like the holy temple is, leaving with what they want and searching for what they need. Lucky has never been in a library before, so this will be a new experience for him. He entered the library and was astounded by how large it was. On the first floor were nothing but old maps and a gift shop. He realized his clothes stank and that he hadn't washed his clothes in a few weeks. So he "borrowed" a T-shirt and some sweatpants from the gift shop.

He made his way to the second floor, and there he found the public reading rooms. He entered the Rose Main Reading Room, and there he found people entranced in their books, each person with a different topic of varying genres. In a room the length of a football field, they sat at desks in neat rows, with lamps to help them read. The room is illuminated by beautiful chandeliers, which makes it easier to see the small painting in the center of the ceiling. A painting of clouds spread out across a morning sky. He looked through the bookshelves, searching for something on evolution. He thought to ask for help, but then he remembered his predicament. Finally, he found it: *From Apes to Humans* by Meridith Halbert, a beginner's book on the theory of evolution and how it relates to humanity. And so, Lucky began to read.

"Evolution is the change and progress of species over several generations through a process called natural selection. Specific genes and traits are naturally selected by a species to ensure the survival of the species, whether for purposes of breeding, hunting, or gathering food. A common example used is how humans and apes share a common ancestor. This common ancestor, through natural selection, splintered off into what we would now call human beings, and others became the great apes. A term regularly used is "survival of the fittest" referring to species that have survived over long periods and have even become apex predators in their respective environments. A Lion, for example, is the apex predator in the savannas of Africa."

Lucky never thought of himself as a predator. He always saw himself as weak and undeserving. "Full of potential," as his teachers would say. But potential for what? He could never decide. The predator inside him was either locked away or was too scared to come out. So he just sat on it, hoping that whatever his potential would come to him like an apple and Newton. Lucky had heard that story somewhere before of some guy named Newton, and an apple fell on his head, and then he created gravity. He looked around the bookshelves to see if they had a book on it. *An Apple Created Gravity* by Gary Bufford is a high school-level book about Isaac Newton.

"Nobody knows for sure if the story is true, but it stands as a testament to Newton's genius and his creativity. Newton was working on a theory of gravity but was trying to figure out how far gravity extended out into the universe. He wondered if perhaps gravity extended all the way to the moon, and that's what was holding it to the Earth's orbit. But one day, while sitting under his apple tree, an apple fell and landed on his head. And it was from this apple that he realized the true nature of gravity. He asked himself, "Why does the apple always fall straight to the ground? It doesn't go up or go sideways; it goes straight down?" He deduced that there must be a gravitational force in the center of the Earth that is drawing objects to it. It doesn't come from the sides of the Earth or extend outwards; rather, things are pulled inwards, and so the Moon's gravitational pull and Earth fight at odds with each other, and they maintain the perfect distance."

Lucky never did think of the Earth much. He was always so consumed in his life—that his problems were so much larger than they actually were. He never considered what was outside of Earth, what else might be lurking out in the darkness of space. He went searching for books about space and found several of them. And so began Lucky's journey. With each thing he learned, it led him down a rabbit hole of further study. There was no one to talk to, no job to work at, and no places to go.

He read about the Big Bang and the origins of the universe, the Milky Way Galaxy, and the thousands of other galaxies outside of it. He read about multiple universe theory and how there might be parallel universes similar to this one but with different variances. That led him to the Bible, the Quran, the Torah, the Vedas, Greek mythology, Norse mythology, Buddhism, etc.

He read the words of Jesus, "A new command I give you: Love one another. As I have loved you, so you must love one another."

He read the words of the Buddha, "Do not dwell in the past, do not dream of the future, concentrate the mind on the present moment."

And he read the words of Krishna, "To those whose minds are always united with Me in loving devotion, I give the divine knowledge by which they can attain Me."

The words of religious teachers led him to the various philosophies of the world: optimism, pessimism, existentialism, absurdism, stoicism, nihilism, atheism, etc.

He read the words of Marcus Aurelius, "It is not death that a man should fear, but he should fear never beginning to live."

He read the words of Albert Camus, "The struggle itself toward the heights is enough to fill a man's heart. One must imagine Sisyphus happy."

And he read the world of Emil Cioran, "What are you waiting for in order to give up?"

He learned about the history of the world, from the Black Plague that spread across Europe in 1346, William Shakespeare was born in 1564, the Battle of Waterloo in 1815, World War II ended in 1945, and Tim Berners-Lee invented the Internet in 1989. Lucky still couldn't get access to the internet. At a certain point, he realized he was starving, but with everyone frozen in time, no one could cook for him. So he found a cookbook in the library and learned how to cook his favorite meal, a cheeseburger, which led him down a path to try to make all sorts of foods that he had always wanted to try but was too scared to take the risk.

***

Fifteen years he spent in that library. Fifteen years of research, practice, of dedication. At the age of 55, he could make sushi from scratch, he could recite every Shakespeare play by heart, and he understood Algebra and even Quantum Mechanics. He could tell you every president of the United States and the wars they helped begin, he can now read at a college level, he can play guitar, and he even learned how to break dance. He wanted to teach himself to drive, but with all the cars on the road and all the people around, he figured it would be unsafe. But he did learn how to ride a bike. *Beginner Bike Riding* by Lavern Hemp taught him all the basics, and he was able to find plenty of great bikes to try out from the people of New York. To keep himself in shape, he would go down to the golf course and hit a couple of balls. Hole-in-ones every time.

He even studied the one thing that might very well save his life: Chemistry. During his eternal Purgatory, he tracked down his old co-worker who sold him the heroin in the first place. He checked the gas station, but he was not there. He went into the back office, looked through the employee records, and found his co-worker's address. He went to their lowly apartment and found out they had come to the same conclusion Lucky had all those months ago. He found his co-worker in a much more compromising position, hanging from the rafters of their bedroom with a noose around their neck. Lucky looked through their drawers, searching for the drug that put him in this cursed state. He waded through loose change and used condoms until he found a bag with a red stamped image of a clock. Before he left, he hugged his co-worker's lifeless, swinging body and returned to the library.

He took the bag of heroin and, with his knowledge of science and chemistry, was able to back-engineer a cure. He had to break into the New York Presbyterian Hospital to do it; they were the only place with the proper equipment. Heroin is a drug that affects the central nervous system. It acts as a depressant, slowing down the person's brain function, affecting their breathing, lowering the temperature and blood pressure, and the heart rate can become erratic. It feels as though time is slowing down. Each person has their own perception of time; when you're stuck in traffic, it feels slower; when you're busy at work, time flies by. Lucky didn't know who created this new strain, but whoever did was able to increase that effect 100-fold. The person who takes the drug has their perception of time slowed down. Time is *literally* slowing down. To everyone else, time is moving normally, but for Lucky, time has stopped. So much so that he could move freely about time itself; it was the reason he could process information so quickly. Since the brain is so relaxed and time is moving at a slower pace, it's able to process information twice as fast, allowing Lucky to retain large amounts of information.

After several more years of work, he created a cure, reversing the effect the drug had on his brain. If the heroin is acting as a depressant, then he needed to create an anti-depressant. One so strong that it would fix the chemical imbalance and make his experience of time in tune with everyone else. For the first time in his dull life, Lucky was excited to be alive. Who knows what applications this knowledge could be used for? What lives he could save? This could be the drug to cure addiction itself. Think of how much money he would make! How successful he would become. He would finally be somebody. He could shove it in the faces of all his teachers and bosses and parents, and show them that he did amount to something. Maybe the one that got away would finally come back. Lucky had finally been Lucky.

But as months rolled by, the cure sat on a shelf in the library, and Lucky continued to read more books. You see, Lucky had become quite content with his predicament. He had no one to bother him, no job to go to, no parents to bug him, and no co-workers to drug him. He had all the food he would ever need until he died, and he had all the time in the world to master any hobby or skill he so desired. Who needs the world? The world gave him nothing but a drug addiction and high expectations. What if the cure didn't work? What if someone steals it? What if it amounted to nothing, and he ended up right back where he started? The rest of the world could wait.

***

After 5 more years, his stubbly face became covered by a bushy beard, his crew cut transformed into long hair that reached to his shoulders, and he was eating plenty of food to fill out his frame, his belly hanging over his sweatpants. His days consisted of studying whatever topic interested him that day; he would take a break to cook some new recipe he wanted to try out, he would hit the golf course, and then go to sleep. Sleeping was weird since the sun never set, and time never flowed. His internal clock had been disrupted ever since his accident. So now he determines when it is time to sleep when he is physically and mentally exhausted, drained of all energy. He's made his home in the basement of the library, blotting out the windows of the basement with black curtains. He sleeps in his sleeping bag. Falling into a blackness deeper than oblivion itself, and he would always wake up feeling refreshed.

But something bothered Lucky. In those 15 years, he did not dream. Before, Lucky also never dreamed. For so long, his head had been filled with nothing, filled with nonsense. And now he was filled with knowledge and wisdom. Surely, this would facilitate some sort of dreams. He became restless. He wondered if this had to do with his internal clock, with it always being sunny out, and his body was confused about what it should do. Regardless, Lucky had to reserve his dreams for the day. And boy, did he ever dream. Since he began his lifelong pursuit of study, he has not only gained knowledge about how the world functions but of the world itself. He had read about the Colosseum of Rome, the Eifel Tower in France, the aurora borealis of Iceland, the Great Wall of China, Stonehenge, the wildlife of Africa, and the pyramids of Egypt. He's read plenty of it, but he has never experienced it. At 60 years old, Lucky had all the time in the world, but it seemed to be running out. Lucky decided, then and there, that he would finally leave that musty library. He would travel the world. He couldn't take a car, train, or plane as he didn't know how to operate any of those things. As skilled as he was, reading about a plane is different than flying one itself. He didn't even want to ride a bike. Lucky decided to walk, to walk the great roads and plains of this Earth, until he had seen it all. Lucky went down to the first floor of the library, and there he found the map room he had dismissed all those years ago. And began to study them, the vast landscapes of this great Earth. With a bag full of perishable foods, a jug filled with water, and hiking gear and clothing he stole from the department store, off he went into the great unknown.

***

Climbing Mount Everest is not as easy as it seems in the novels. Wearing a thick parka, heavy snow pants, two scarves around his face, a soft beanie, and waterproof boots, Lucky had read all about his predecessors, the equipment they used, the preparations they took, the conditions they faced, and the horrors they saw. Everest is home to over 200 lost souls who tried and failed to reach the summit, the protocol being to leave the bodies. And Lucky saw some along his journey, a grim reminder. As he reached the top, as he had done for the 10th time in over 10 years, he couldn't help but feel hollow this time around. He had done it all. He traveled to Rome and explored the nooks and crannies of the coliseum; in France, he climbed to the very top of the Eiffel Tower; at the highest mountain peak in Iceland, he witnessed the aurora borealis, he walked the entire length of the Great Wall of China in an entire day, he prayed at Stonehenge in England, and he petted lions in Africa. He had traveled to Egypt and explored the inner chambers of the Great Pyramid of Giza, learning its ancient secrets. He ate the food of every country he visited, learned their culture, studied their language, read their literature, practiced their dances, orchestrated their music, and felt their fears and joys and sorrows. Every new country, traveling by boats he had "borrowed" from wealthy yacht owners or sometimes from fishermen who needed to make a daily catch in order to survive. He boated through weathering storms and massive waves, always making sure to stockpile enough food and water, and he would reach wherever he intended. He walked vast distances, resting only when necessary, camping out in the vast wilderness, the plains of Africa, or the tundra of the Antarctic.

He was a master of his domain. Never worrying about money or resources, he was free. Free as any man had ever been in the history of the world. But it was all not enough. And now standing on top of Mount Everest, at 70 years old, he realized how hollow he felt. He had let himself go. His beard went down to his knees, his hair down to his butt crack, he smelled bad, his teeth had gone yellow, and he was skin and bones. All that he had accomplished would never be good enough if there weren't anyone around to share it with. That special someone. The one that got away. Lucky knew he didn't have much longer to live; he had a good 10 years left, maybe. It could be tomorrow for all he knew. It was a good life he was walking through, but he knew that it was time to start living it.

***

New York City had remained the same since he last saw it, but I guess why would it change? Everything had been exactly as he had left; even the piles and piles of books he had never read were still where they were in the Rose Reading Room of the New York Public Library. The people were still frozen like shadows of an atomic bomb, their stories never coming to a natural conclusion. A rat is trying to scurry away into a drain, crowds of people are stepping on and off of the subway, a taxi driver gives a pedestrian the middle finger, there's a drunk woman pissing on the street corner, and an art student holds up a sign, "The End Is Near".

He made a quick visit to his coworker, the one who sold him the drugs, the one who started it all. He was still hanging there on the rafters, on the edge of life and death. Lucky left a flower for him as a token of appreciation. It was Lucky's decisions that brought him to where he was, but he had to acknowledge the friends who helped him along the way.

"Thank you, my friend," he said aloud. And then left the apartment for the final time.

He found her address in the phone book, the cell towers still weren't working, and Lucky threw his phone into the Pacific Ocean several years ago. She was still there. If she wasn't there, if she was off in another country, or if she was lost in the sea of New York, Lucky would never have found her. But I guess he had some time if he really wanted to. She just got out of the shower, standing in front of her dresser mirror, brushing her wet hair, and draped in a shower robe. She's beautiful. He wouldn't want her any other way, pure and natural. He had to break the door down with a fire axe, but he needed to see her. Her luxury apartment, with a view over Manhattan, a fireplace in the living room, a toaster with four slots, a king-size bed, and a shower head with the hardest of streams. All her rich boyfriend's doing. Lucky remembers seeing him on the TV. CEO of some company that does something or the other, Lucky didn't care. He cared about her. He cared about if Mr. CEO was treating her right, if she was happy, if she was fed, and if her needs were met. He loved her and always did. But Lucky was older now, and she was still so young. Lucky could've had her years ago, but he wasn't the same man as he is now. It's too late. Too late for love but not too late for life. He left her apartment and headed back out to the streets of New York.

Lucky went back to Times Square, the first stop he ever took on his perilous journey. He stood atop the red stairs again and looked over the people as he did all those years ago. He was scared. He wanted to stay here at this moment in time. He'd been living inside a photo for most of his life, even before the incident. He was stagnant, scared to move forward, always staying in place. Even before the drugs, he was frozen in time. All of that was over now. Pulling his hand out of his pocket, he pulled out the antidote, the one he had made in the public library with the knowledge he had learned. Twenty-five years of knowledge was about to be put into practice, and the nightmare finally ends. Who knows what he would make of the world; who knows of the people he would meet, the friends he would make, and the lovers he would hold. His whole life ahead of him.

Lucky injected the green liquid into his veins with the syringe. Funny, this all started with a needle, and it all ends with a needle. He knew something was wrong when he felt how cold he was. His heart began to beat faster and faster. He could see time beginning to flow, the ice cream falling to the ground, people crossing the sidewalk, and cars moving along with the traffic.

On the stairwell of an old New York apartment, old lady Karuthers is sitting on the steps after a sudden burst of pain in her face, almost as if some invisible force had slapped her. Her groceries have all fallen out of her bags and are now strewn about the stairs.

"Ow, my face!" she screams.

In the New York Public Library, the staff is perplexed as to how piles of books were pulled from their shelves and placed into neat piles in the blink of an eye. They also wonder how tons of food scraps, empty plates and cups, utensils, golf clubs, chemistry materials, and sleeping bags all ended up in the basement.

A girl in a high-rise New York apartment is brushing her hair after a long hot shower and recounting her high school days and the strange boy named Lucky who had fancied her. She never thought about him, but for some strange reason, he just popped into her brain. She wondered how he was doing. But just then, her boyfriend ran in from the other room.

"Babe! What happened to the front door?!" he screams.

They both rush over to the front door, only to find that it has been chopped through and caved in.

Life began to flash before Lucky's eyes, and suddenly, it all came crashing to an end. Maybe he mixed the antidote wrong. Maybe it had gone bad from sitting on the shelf all those years. Or maybe after all this time, before time had slowed down, he had overdosed on that heroin, and the slowing of time was the only thing that was saving his life. Regardless, time had officially caught up with him. His heart stopped, the synapses of his brain stopped firing, and the blood stopped flowing. His body went limp, and he crashed down the red stairs, bumping into pedestrians. A crowd began to form around, wondering what happened. Many comments were thrown about drugs or alcohol and homelessness. Some thought he was faking; others pulled out their phone to record. Only a few called the cops, and when they finally arrived, Lucky was placed onto a stretcher and carted off in an ambulance to New York Presbyterian Hospital. Where he would be declared a John Doe, cremated, and then thrown in the dumpster.

DAY

32

I remembered more today. I still can't remember my name, but I'm starting to remember who I am. I lived with my father until I was 10 years old. He took on the burden of raising me alone after my mother was transported to the asylum. He was a respectable man. He owned a grocery store in the New Brunswick, Canada, region. Everyone knew him for his kindness and his service to the community.

He was a God-fearing man. Every Sunday, we went to church, and every night, we said our prayers. He instilled two principles in me at a young age: to work hard and to always listen. As long as I followed those two simple rules, he showed me kindness and showed me mercy. My father liked me, but I don't think he loved me. I think he saw me as a burden, something that was dropped upon him out of nowhere, and now he must carry me around out of responsibility alone.

One day, he was working on his hovercycle. He loved that damn thing more than he loved me. Imagine an old motorcycle, but where the wheels are, inductors that create a powerful magnetic field take their place. One of the inductors was malfunctioning, and he couldn't figure out what was wrong. He decided to take a break, and he went inside to take a nap. "Don't touch the bike. Ever," he said to me.

While he was asleep, I went into the garage to check out the bike. I was already the smartest in my class, with straight A's and all. My father pushed me to study hard; he didn't want me to end up in the grocery store like him. So, by the time I was 10, I had the intelligence of a college graduate.

I took a look at the bike and poked around with my father's tools to try and fix the inductor. I was able to fix it, and while he was still asleep, I took his bike for a little joy ride. I don't know where I got the confidence from; I was not a rambunctious kid. But it's one of my best memories. I'm riding the bike on the highway, the wind blowing hard in my face, my hair whipping back. In a car, you don't realize how often the temperature changes, how intense the smell of the open air is, and just how fragile you really are. If I fell off the bike, I surely would have died, but I didn't care. It was one of the only times in my life when I truly felt free.

By the time I got back, my father was waiting for me in the garage. I thought for sure he was going to be happy that I fixed the bike, and he was going to be proud of me for my resourcefulness. He didn't do that. Instead, he punched me in the face and broke my nose. Maybe it's because I didn't listen to him, or maybe he couldn't handle his son being better than him. From that moment, I lost his love, and I lost his mercy. He sent me to St. Mary's Orphanage the following year.

"The whole world is an angry place."

RAISE CAIN

The first thing I do in the morning is shift my head over to my nightstand and unplug my phone. I have a perfect view of that delicious blue screen while remaining as comfortable as possible. As I scroll through all of the brain rot, that's when the reports start to roll in.

"-asteroid passing by Earth today-"
"-one of a kind event-"
"-unsure of the consequences-"
"-God has sent us a gift-"
"-the end times are upon us-"
"-make sure to follow for more-"

You can always thank the internet for providing the opinions of every single living being, for better or for worse. I scroll through video after video of people around the world looking up at the sky. A small asteroid with a fiery tail slowly makes its way across the Earth's atmosphere. I remember hearing something about that asteroid, but I've been so busy the days all blur together. And speaking of work, I've been staring so long at my phone that 2 hours have gone by. I'm already late.

I get out of bed and head to the bathroom. On my way, I hastily grab a pair of underwear from the clean laundry basket, it might have been the dirty one, but there's no time for further inspection. I just slip them on and hope for the best. My hair is short enough to where I can just wet it down with water from the sink, and I can quickly brush my teeth in a few minutes and slap on some deodorant. No shower is required. I then run out of the bathroom and head over to my closet, where I have a few white collared shirts, a few pairs of black pants, and a few different colored ties. I decided to go with the black tie today. I slip on my pants and tuck in my shirt, and as I'm tying my tie, I begin to hear the ruckus going on outside.

I open my window and look outside to find that the neighbors are furious. Not at me, but at each other. I've seen Pam and Johnny fight before, but not like this. The screaming is so loud you would think it would be blasting over a megaphone. They're screaming in each other's faces on the front lawn. Johnny is about to burst a blood vessel, and Pam is holding the pink flamingo lawn ornament in her hand, and I swear she's about to bash him upside the head with it. And their daughter Annie is sitting on the front steps of the house, crying her eyes out. Her face is as red as a tomato, and the tears are streaming like a lawn sprinkler. I get distracted by the arguing when I see a chair fly through the window of the house next door. In the house next to that, a car backs up hard out of the driveway without even opening the garage door. Bits of hardwood and plastic come flying out onto the road, and a little sports car peels out, leaving behind dust and tire marks as it makes its way out of the neighborhood. I look to my left and see the neighbor's tree on fire; I look to my right and see a hole in the neighbor's wall where the oven used to be. I'm worried that something is going on, but then I get a call from work asking me where I am. I finish getting ready, but I have no time for coffee or breakfast. I get in my car and head to work.

***

"-reports of strange behavior-"
"-riots in the streets-"
"-bouts of anger and violence-"
"-the meteor might be the cause-"
"-virus-"

I keep changing the station on the radio, but nothing good is on. They don't play music anymore; it's just ads and people talking about celebrities. Can't a guy listen to a good tune on his way to work? Especially on a hot day like today? I must've woken up on the wrong side of the bed or something because I'm angrier than a monkey without a banana. Sorry, that's an old saying my mom used to toss around.

"Scientists have confirmed that the asteroid named Iram is causing the bouts of anger that seems to have infected the entire world. Iram was seen several months ago by the Asteroid Terrestrial-impact Alert System (ATLAS). Scientists determined that the asteroid would not make impact with Earth and that it would simply pass over it on August 28th, during this hot summer day. Well, it seems that the asteroid has brought more than a beautiful sight to see, as the entire world has gone into a frenzy. Reported bouts of anger in the workplace, riots in the streets, looting, road rage, increased crime, and gun violence. All over the world, treaties are being broken, alliances destroyed, wars are being broken out, genocides ensuing, and threats of nuclear war are more imminent than ever. The Center for Disease Control (CDC) has determined that there is indeed some sort of virus in the air that was carried by the asteroid and is now raining down on the Earth as it passes over. The dubbed "Iram Virus" is not infectious, is not spread through bodily contact or fluids, nor does it cause sickness or death. The virus simply stimulates the hypothalamus in the brain, and it increases epinephrine production, which is a chemical produced when you are angry. The virus causes extreme bouts of anger over time, but scientists have determined that the virus does not live very long here on Earth. Seemingly unable to stand the heat of the sun, and dissolving after a couple of hours. Therefore, scientists theorize that once Iram passes by the end of today, the virus should be wiped out within a few days, which is why the CDC is recommending people stay in their homes, social distance, wear face masks, and use hand sanitizer after touching surfaces. Stay tuned for more updates."

I turn off the radio. I don't have time for a virus; I'm late for work as it is. It makes us angry? So what. The whole world is an angry place. Wrathful and vengeful, it is the core of the human spirit. Look at this; it's a beautiful day out. Sun shining and not a cloud in sight, the sky so blue it makes you want to dive right in. You feel cured, like you've been sick your whole life until the sun came out. The sun increases your serotonin, gives you a nice color, and gives you a sense that everything will be okay. It's like believing in God. You look at the forests along the highway, and the trees are such a deep green. And if you take your eyes off the road for one second, you can see a babbling brook. It's like some secluded paradise that you can't reach; it's been put off-limits to you by the highway patrol. It's probably why there are so many potholes, because the police officers and road construction workers are too busy swimming in this fountain of youth that we normal folk aren't privileged enough to experience.

All of that is going on, and look at what people are doing. As I'm driving, I'm looking out on the highway, and all I see is people fighting each other. The traffic has come to a standstill, and people are hopping out of their cars and just mauling each other. Some guy has an old lady in a headlock, two chicks are going at each other with their fists, and a dog is thrown into the forest cause he has the guy's toupee in his mouth. I drive around it all, not really caring if I hit someone. I'm pretty sure I did because when I ran over a bump, a lot of screaming and yelling increased after that. But I just kept on driving.

I pull off the highway and head into downtown, where things are so much worse. Local businesses with windows smashed from aluminum bats, Molotov cocktails thrown into antique stores, looting of bread and milk, hand sanitizer, face masks, flat-screen TVs, the newest phones, the latest game consoles and VR headsets, jewelry, cash, good old fashioned loot, and pillage. People are lying dead or dying, faces bashed in, curb-stomped mouths with teeth strung about like snowflakes on the concrete, and blood splattered against the white lines in the road like Jackson Pollock. People beat to exhaustion, their faces swollen with black eyes, agape mouths with gap teeth, and sidewalks of bodies like wilted flowers. Some were even in the street, which is annoying cause I have to drive over them like road kill.

Suddenly, running out of the alleyways in groups of five are ravenous, loudmouth packs of moochers waiving pistols and knives in the air. They're screaming and threatening each other in the middle of the crosswalk. I hit the brakes and come to a screeching halt; they don't even notice me. I honk the horn, and now, suddenly, the guns are pointed at me. I slam on the accelerator, smashing into a couple of these thugs, and as I whiz past, bullets smash into my windshield, and stray bits of glass land in my lap and in the passenger seat. They're shooting at me, and all I do is scream, "GO TO HELL!" This world's falling apart since the day it began, I'll tell you that. It's not just the asteroid. This stuff has been boiling underneath the surface; this just finally gave them the excuse to let it burst.

***

I finally arrive at the office. The grey building filled with all the grey people. Their shape has no form or function, they simply exist as this lingering entity that you don't give a second thought about as you pass by it. It's just there; it always has been, and it always will be. A permanent fixture tethered to this Earth, unsure of its origins, its purpose, and what they produce for the world. The building and the people are one and the same. In the 10 years I've worked at Investicorp, I've never come to know the people or the work that I am doing. I genuinely don't know what the company does or my role in it. I sit at my computer for 8 hours, file reports, and create spreadsheets of profits and margins. I have weekly meetings about these profits and what we could be doing to increase them, but I don't know what it is that we produce. And in the very few conversations I've had with my co-workers, none of them seem to know what the hell is going on. They don't care. And you know what; I don't care. I don't get paid enough to care. I just sit there, and take it, or else I don't eat and I lose my house.

I park my car in the Investicorp parking lot, and one of my tires popped from the bullets, so the metal drags along the concrete, screeching and spitting out sparks. I step out of my car; my white collared shirt is covered in blood, and my tie is all scratched up along with my face. I'm sweating hard from the heat, and it's making the blood get in my eyes; I have to wipe it with my shirt, which gets more blood on me. I think I hit the accelerator a little too hard cause I have a cramp in my leg, so I limp into the office. Everything looks calm; no receptionist at the front desk. I take the elevator, and it's not till I get to my floor, the fourth floor, when I see the ensuing chaos. Papers fly across the room, and people are running in a panic; they're shouting into the phones, throwing staplers, and punching computer screens. Some were cowering under their desks, shaking and crying, and others were standing on top of them, waving their hands in the air like some Bolivian rain dance.

"The stocks are plummeting!" someone shouts.

"The shareholders will be pissed!" another voice screams.

Stocks? Shareholders? This is all news to me and news that I'm willing to ignore. I scramble past unconscious bodies across the floor in order to get to my desk and start logging my hours onto my computer. I try to drown out the screaming, but then one of them starts howling at the desk behind me. I get up, and I'm about to chop him in the throat, when another one of these neanderthals has the same idea as me. I slowly sit back down, watching the events unfold as the howling baboon is tossed to the floor. The two get on top of each other, heaps of bloody flesh. Soon, a circle begins to form, and the two of them are wrestling around on the carpet, giving themselves rug burns. It's a full-on blood bath. Eventually, one of them gets on top of the other, and they grab a rock paperweight from someone's desk and bash in their skulls. It's over as quickly as it begins. The chaos continues as it was. I decide to just ignore it and return to my work.

***

By the 7th hour, things have started to calm down. During my break, I checked my phone and saw more videos of the world plunging into a similar chaos. But now it seems that the asteroid only has a couple of hours left until it leaves the Earth's orbit, and according to radio reports, most of the virus has died off. Only a small trace of it remains, and the violent fever that has ravaged the Earth has already slowed down. I only have an hour left of my shift, and I go home and forget about this horrible day. As I have the days previous.

I take a glance around to see what the others are doing, as I have tuned them out for quite some time. It seems they have all gathered around a fire made from ties, skirts, and possibly some coffee grounds from the break room. The air smells of burnt coffee. One of them is chanting, speaking in tongues; the others are enraptured by the rambling. I can only deduce that they are telling a story of some kind; what it is, I don't know.

I'm just about to finish logging in my hours, but then here he comes. Ken from HR. I'm surprised I haven't seen him sooner, considering this whole situation breaks every single company policy. He runs over to the group huddled by the fire, yelling at them, babbling like an idiot in some incoherent, made-up language no one can understand. All the others know is that he is angry, and they begin to feel frightened. He then makes his way over to me, standing over my desk, looking me up and down, sizing me up like some sort of predator. He doesn't say a word to me; he just stands there, breathing heavily into my face; the stench of old eggs comes from his mouth, and stabs my nose with malicious intent.

It's only then that I notice his red tie. And I don't know why, but that tie really pisses me off. After all I've seen today, all I've experienced is the destruction of humanity, the harming of others, and the complete lack of decency. But for some reason, his tie is the final straw. It's too…red. Too vibrant, too in your face. It feels amplified, like all of the light in the world is fixed upon this tie. I feel like a bull in Spain, and Ken is waiving his tie, taunting me. Mocking me. I can't stand it any longer. I grab his tie and tug it down hard so his head slams into the corner of the desk. It makes a cut on his forehead, and blood starts pouring down his face. He falls to the ground, and the sound of his collapsing body alerts the tribe of coworkers. They see what I have done, and they're not happy about it. It riles them up; their frowns turn to anger, eyebrows furrowed, sleeves rolled up, blouses torn off; it's about to be like a battle from the Stone Ages. They rush me. I grab a pencil and jam it into the first ape that lunges for my throat, and as he falls to the ground, I'm already jamming my thumbs into a secretary's eyes. We fall to the ground, but they soon scramble to their feet and start kicking my body. I fight through the pain of broken ribs and stand up with a troglodyte on my back. I carry him and slam him into the nearest wall, leaving a human-shaped indent. He lets go of my back, and I kick him in the face. The others lead the charge, and I fight off each one with moves I learned from midnight Bruce Lee movies. Chops to the throat, kicks to the groin, punches to the nose, I even manage to sweep the legs of someone. But I trip over myself, and soon I'm overcome.

They lift me off the ground and carry me as if I stage-dived at a rock concert. I scream, I kick, I punch, anything I can to shake their grasp. But it's no use. The demons have me, and they want to drag me to hell. They carry me to the stairwell and bring me down all the way to the ground floor. They drag me outside, chanting to some foreign God. And me, their sacrifice. It was there, out in the Investicorp parking lot, where the heathens threw me to the ground and began the ritual. My arms, my legs, and my head, each appendage grabbed by a person in the crowd. And then they pulled, and they pulled, and they pulled, the flesh beginning to tear, cartilage split, muscle torn, and bones separate. I am in agony, and all I can think about is that damn red tie. A loud rip and pop echoes, and my torso lands on black asphalt. The crowd is tossing around my arms and legs. Some are even taking small bites out of it. My head is tossed to the side, landing in a small bush by the entrance. I'm looking up towards the sky. They say a human head can see for up to 30 seconds when decapitated. I can confirm that is true. As the neurons in my brain stop firing, my vision goes black, and all that was once ever me absorbs back into the Earth; I see the asteroid flying through the sky. It becomes smaller and smaller and smaller, until finally it is nothing more than a speck, and then…gone. Blipped out of existence in the blink of an eye. It has left the Earth, and with it, it carries the souls of a hundred thousand dead. Flying off into the cosmos into uncharted territory. Hopefully, somewhere better than here.

DAY

89

I remember the orphanage. The wooden floors creaked, the smell of mold filled with air, spiders nested in their webs on the ceiling rafters, and winter winds made their way through every broken window and every crack through these barren walls.

I remember a small altar for prayer. A solitary statue of Mary holding Jesus, dead, having just come down from the cross. I hated my father, but prayer was something I had fond memories of. It was quiet, it was relaxing, and it gave me a chance to commune with something far greater than myself. And on days when it felt the loneliest, on the days when the other children were relentless in their mockings when my "caretakers" could barely look me in the eye, when potential parents couldn't be bothered to glance me over, and when it felt that God had abandoned me; I prayed at the statue. For hours and hours, I prayed. For 8 long years, I prayed. But he remained silent. Was God punishing me for my misgivings? Was all of this really perhaps my fault? Well, if this was all really God's doing, well then I wanted no part in his grand design.

At 18, I was released from my "prison". And after those 8 years, I had lost all faith. It was beaten out of me, and I was subjugated to a hopeless society. But it wasn't all for nothing. Because of my outcast state, that only pushed me further to excel in my studies. The only good thing my father ever taught me. I received the highest marks in the state, and I was accepted into Harvard University. There, my love for science was nurtured. I partook in every subject and its related fields. I looked upon the world with cold hard facts and logic, and the only person to rely upon was myself. As it always had been and will always continue to be. That's when I realized that my time might be better spent off-world. After I graduated, I applied at NASA and was accepted.

"What do you want me to be?"

LA PETITE MORT

She cowers on the motel bed, trying to hide herself behind fluffy white pillows. She's beautiful, naked, 18 maybe, I didn't really ask. The motel is fine enough. A black light would tell a different story, but the less I know the better. All I know is what I can see, cigarette butts from previous tenants, grease stains from the fried chicken joint down the road, itchy sheets that are eggshell but were definitely once white, and a bathroom that smells of mildew with stray hairs on the shower walls.

I tuck my dress shirt back into my pants and zip them up, and I adjust my tie in the bathroom mirror while simultaneously checking my face for laugh lines or zits. Beauty isn't forever, but we can maintain it while it lasts. I turn on the faucet and give my face a good rinse, and I pat dry it with the hand towel. Then I hear a small whimper coming from the bedroom, and I step out of the bathroom.

"I didn't hurt you too badly, did I?" I comfortingly ask.

She wipes a tear from her eye and then the blood from her lips.

"It's been a hot minute; I get a little rowdy when I haven't had any. But you're just what I needed," I say as I wink at her.

Before I make my exit, I put a couple extra hundreds on the nightstand. I always make sure to tip the waitstaff. I leave her there; she knows her way out. Usually, they want to stay for a few minutes, have a good cry, and reevaluate their life. Maybe they even kill themselves. Who knows?

"Keep the change," I say.

I exit the hotel and feel the crisp night air across my skin. I stand there and soak it in. It feels so good, but I can't help but wonder if these winds are in my favor or if these are the winds of change.

***

The little death, that's what they call it. Which is ironic because it's the only time I feel alive. I've been chasing the orgasm ever since I experienced my first wet dream at 13 years old. That first time is always your best, you've never felt anything like it before, and no matter how hard you try, you can never find it again. I've had all kinds of women, I've had madams, I've been gagged and beaten, and I've had near-death experiences, and it's never been as good as that first time.

My usual walk through my local Red Light District seemed fruitless as I looked upon the pick of the litter. The usual crowds of drug whores and transvestites lay about the cobblestone road. The red lights warm my heart; they're the most beautiful sight. The red lights envelop the entirety of the street, bathing us in the blood of the universe. If it weren't for the smell of homeless piss and the garbage lining the streets, I would feel right at home.

Home is something I've never had. My father left me when I was a kid, and my mother raised me on her own. Well, as best as she could with a belly full of scotch. By the time I was 18, I left her and started working in real estate. Now I make 6 figures, I live in a nice apartment, and I can have any woman I want. The problem is that women don't know a good, high-value man when they see one. So I figured, to hell with love. Who needs it? If women don't want me, I'll make them want me.

As I walk, faces go here and there. I see familiars, mostly newbies. I have my favorites, those comfort foods that I can't help but munch into. But mostly, it's the five-star meals, the succulent steaks, the prime ribs, the fresh lobsters, and the beautiful animals that I can't help but conquer. They all beckon and call to me like sirens on the open sea. I needed something different, something unique. And then I saw her.

A beautiful blonde woman, 5 ft. 6 in., 2 inches shorter than me, beautiful body with curvy hips, a flat stomach, a fine ass, and legs that go all the way up. Wearing a skin-tight pink dress, black heels, and red ruby lips. The most beautiful woman I've ever seen. She looks like a Barbie doll, or at least she will be when I have my way with her.

"I haven't seen you around here?" I say.

"I'm new," she says.

No sexy expression, just a resting bitch face. Honestly, I like it. She knows how to entice a man. "Want me, but don't want me" kind of vibe.

"Well, I'm something of a regular around here, and I like to break in the newbies. You wanna find a room somewhere?" I ask.

She takes me by the hand and leads me to the Four Winds Motel, the local spot where all the action happens. We enter the motel, and Al is at the front desk.

"Hey, Al. Sad news. The wife kicked me out of the house. Such a shame, right? I need a room for the night. And this pretty little number here is gonna keep me company. You know how scared I get when I'm all alone," I say.

Al owns the motel. He knows me pretty well, considering I bring him a significant amount of his business. I'm not married. He knows I'm not married. Even the girl knows I'm not married. But I can't walk up to the front desk talking about prostitutes. Never know who's listening.

"A shame is right. A crying shame. Room 403. Sleep tight," says Al unenthusiastically.

He hands me the key, and Bob's your uncle. Up the stairs we go, up to the heaven that is room 403. I've been in all the rooms at this motel except this one. A momentous occasion. I wonder if I get a T-shirt or something. I'll have to ask Al on the way out. I put the key in the lock and hear the shifting of gears until the door swings open, and the smell of bleach stings my nostrils. That's the charm of the Four Winds; it's clean in a disgusting way. Even though the sheets are washed, the beds are made, the toilet scrubbed, the shower wiped, and the carpet vacuumed, you can't help but feel disgusted. Whenever I lay in one of those beds, I can smell the freshness of the fabric softener, but the way my legs and back itch, the way my skin turns red, says otherwise. When I sit on the toilet, my stomach feels sick, and when I use the shower, I have to shampoo twice. Ever normal on the outside but festering with sick on the inside. Teeming to the surface, waiting to burst like a teenage pimple.

It's like sex. Every person walks around ever normal, with their designer clothes, their fat lattes, their fancy jobs, and stacks of green paper. But underneath all that is an insatiable desire to fuck everything in their sight. Unprohibited by the guilt and the shame, humanity would fuck itself to death in one lustful act of destruction. It's all we would do. Food would become meaningless; water would be disgusting; love would be impossible, just our base need to procreate and chase the La Petite Mort.

70

We enter into room 403. I go straight to the bed so I can sit down and take off my shoes. I'm looking at her, and it's not until now that I realize she doesn't have a purse, no wallet, no phone, no makeup kits, nothing. Usually, these whores have a toolbox and medical kit worth of supplies, but she's a light traveler, I guess. Not much of a conversationalist either. She hasn't said a goddamn word since I picked her up. At first, I liked it, but now not so much. She's all intense. No fun at all, and definitely not a turn-on. She walks into the room like a robot, slowly and methodically walking to the foot of the bed, greeting me with dead eyes.

"Alright, toots. You should probably take your clothes off. I'm not much of a gentleman, so don't expect me to take them off for you," I say.

"What do you want me to be?" she asks.

"Uh, I want you to be undressed and on this bed yesterday," I say as I start unbuckling my belt.

"What do you want me to be?" she repeats.

"Lady, I'm not into the whole roleplay thing. I'm not looking for anything fancy, alright. Just get undressed already, and I'll do all the work," I respond, getting a little annoyed now.

"What do you want me to be?" she repeats for the third time.

I stand up in anger. I walk over to her and grab her arm.

"Are you fucking deaf or something? I said—"

She cuts me off by grabbing my arm and twisting it hard.

She doesn't even flinch as she twists my arm to the point where it almost breaks. I'm screaming in agony, begging her to stop, watching as my skin twists and torts, hoping to God I don't see bone pop out at any minute. She bends it so far that I fall to my knees, giving myself some leverage.

"Okay! Alright! I'm sorry! Whatever you want to do!" I scream.

She finally lets go, and I fall backward against the bed. I'm holding my arm, focusing so much on the pain that it takes me a second before I notice that before my very eyes, she begins to change shape. Her skin folds in on itself, changing shades of color, and even the amount of arm and leg hair changes. Like a chameleon, the color of her hair changes immediately to whatever she desires; same goes for the color of her eyes. I can even see her perfectly white teeth, changing height, length, and width, along with her hair, her finger, and toenails. Even her clothes begin to change, transforming from a pink skin-tight dress to a stunning, long-flowing sun dress. I love sundresses. Everything changes until she transforms from a beautiful white blonde to a bombshell black woman with thick black hair, thick thighs, and a thick ass.

"Holy—" I begin to say.

"What do you want me to be?" she says again.

I understand. I should be mortified; I should be running and screaming to the hills; I should fucking kill her or whatever this thing is. But I can't bring myself to do anything. My mind is filled with the endless possibilities. Who needs a $100 skank when I can have whoever I want, whenever I want?

"How much?" I ask.

"$5,000 a night," she replies.

"...Marilyn Monroe," I say.

And before my very eyes, she turns herself into Marilyn Monroe. Down to the white flowing dress, the ruby red lips, the bright blonde hair, and those delicious skinny legs.

"Rita Hayworth."

***

Years pass by, and I'm seeing her every month. I'm craving her like drugs, like a child who tastes candy for the very first time. She's the most exquisite creature I've ever seen. She's taken control of my life. All of my money goes to her. I got fired from my job; I moved out of my apartment and into a trailer home. All the money I make is from unemployment. The only food I buy is ramen packets; I sold all my furniture, all my DVDs, and game consoles; I even sold my baseball card collection from when I was a kid. I only drink tap water, I don't go to the bars, I don't go out at all. I'm all hers.

At first, it was Hollywood actresses; then, it was famous musicians, athletes, and porn stars. Then it was women I had crushes on in the past, old girlfriends, acquaintances, teachers, classmates, coworkers, baristas, nurses, then it was people I would just pass by on the street. And then sometimes the most beautiful person would pop into my brain, somewhere deep in the recesses of my brain, where my darkest and wildest fantasies are stored, a person would be crafted into the ether, and she would bring them to life for me to love. Years of this, thousands upon thousands of dollars, wasted, lost, all in the name of this exquisite creature I don't even know the name of.

"No names," she said.

"Fine by me," I replied.

I asked her if she had other clients, and she told me I was the only one. I didn't believe her, but it sure damn made me feel good. For someone new, she sure acted like a professional. She knew all the moves, all the right spots. It was like telepathy or something; she knew exactly what I liked without me having to tell her. I was always exhausted and drained after each session, and she barely broke a sweat. She could go all night if she wanted to.

"So, where are you from exactly? Outer space?" I asked in all seriousness.

"That's none of your concern," she replied.

"Well, I figure I ought to know something. I mean, what if you give me space aids or something?" I asked with genuine concern.

"I am clean. And that is all you need to know," she said sternly.

And that was the end of it. It all felt so good that I didn't really see the need to bother with it. I soon asked around with the other girls about her. I wasn't seeing them, mind you; another woman hasn't felt the same since her. I asked them when she started working, where she came from, what her story was. But nobody seemed to know who I was talking about. And I realized, that she would be constantly changing her form, so nobody would really know who she is. Nobody knows her true form, her true face if she indeed has one. It seems that she just showed up one day and started working the streets. No one knows what her name is, where she came from, who she works for, and what her deal is. She is a mystery, and that makes me want her so much more.

It's September now, and the autumn breeze produces goosebumps on my bony arms and legs. I'm a skeleton decoration barely clinging to your front door. But boy, do I scare away the children. My eyes are sunken into my skull, my teeth are so yellow, my breath is like rotting meat, and my hair is falling out. I sold all of my nice clothes, and all I had left was a pair of old jeans and a T-shirt. It's not Halloween yet, but it should be cause it would give me an excuse for why I look so ridiculous. The babes in the Red-Light District give me the strangest looks. They used to look at me with lust-filled eyes and seductive lips, but now it's as if I have the plague. Like the slightest glance of my twisted features will cause convulsing and contusions. I am a shell of my former self.

I find her where she always is. On the street corner, bathed in red light.

"How will I know it's you?" I asked her once.

"You will know," she answered.

And sure enough, I did know. She looked nothing like when I first met her. She's now Asian, chubby, with lots of fat on the legs, a large stomach, huge breasts, dimples on her cheeks, long flowing black hair, a short black skirt, and a white tank top. She's gorgeous. I stumble on over, with my lanky frame, and address my holy goddess.

"Hey…I, uh, you're new, right?" I seductively say.

"I'm new," she responds.

"Oh, well, I uh, I'm a regular junkyard cat, and uh… Hey, can we just knock this shit off already? We've been seeing each other so long we don't have to do this every time," I charmingly say.

She doesn't even look in my direction. You get to a point in this business when you can tell they're getting sick of you. They know you inside and out; they know your likes and dislikes, your strengths and weaknesses, and your failures and successes. It's like a real relationship with none of the commitment. I'd been working her like a workhorse during the harvest season, and some girls get sick of you after a while, even if you do have the funds. But I can't let her go. I refuse to let someone else have her. The thought of others riding my prized stallion makes me sick. We have a connection, she and I.

I can take care of her. I can love her like no one else can. I barely know her; she's never revealed anything to me, but that doesn't matter. We can have a good life together, I can protect her, I know I can. This is my second chance. I'm gonna ask her to come with me tonight. I can find a job; I can change. I'll do anything for her. All she has to do is say yes. But before I can do any of that, she takes my hand and leads me to the Four Winds Motel. Our special place.

"Room 403," says Al.

Room 403. The room that started it all. The one that we have gone to every night since. Al and I dropped the shtick pretty quickly, and whenever I would walk to the front desk, he'd have the keys ready in hand. The room still looks the same: the carpet has been vacuumed, the bleach stings my nostrils all the way from the bathroom, and the shades by the window have a mysterious stain from previous tenants.

I take her hand and lead her from the door to the bed. I sit down, and she stays standing up. I look up to her like my queen, and she looks down upon me like her peasant. We just stare at each other for a moment, me with admiration, she with disgust.

"What would you like me to be?" she asks, as she always does.

"In a minute, doll. Listen, we've been doing this for a long time. And I'm running out of money. But I know there's a connection between us. You can feel the electricity. And I'm asking you, please, if you would be with me. I can take care of you. I can love you. Like, for *real* love you. I know I don't know you, but you know me. And I can get to know you. We can navigate this crazy world together. What do ya say?" I ask her.

She stands there, almost lifeless. Her eyelids lower, her lips straighten, her jaw relaxes, and her limbs stiffen and straighten. She really does look like a Barbie doll now. She almost looks bored.

"What do you want me to be?" she asks again.

"I don't want you to be anything right now. I want you to answer me," I say.

"What do you want me to be?" she asks a third time.

"I want you to be with me!" I scream.

"What do you want me to be?" she asks a fourth time.

"WHATEVER I WANT YOU TO BE!" I scream.

Everything goes silent, and the air is still. She looks at me with those unmoving eyes. She takes a few steps back, never breaking her gaze. Before me, she transforms into that of the cute blonde she was when I first met her.

"No, that's not... I'm sorry," I say.

She then transforms into the black woman when she first revealed her powers to me.

"No, sweetheart, I don't want any of this. I want you," I plead.

In a cacophony of madness, she transforms rapidly into the many forms she's undertaken for me. Celebrities, musicians, athletes, porn stars, friends, family, acquaintances, old girlfriends, lovers, one-night stands, strangers on the street. All of the different races, ethnicities, colors, creeds, fat, skinny, short, tall, big tits, small ass, with lingerie, tight dresses, small dresses, pajamas, skinny jeans, sweatpants, sweatshirts, tank tops, jumpsuits, and every combination in-between. Everything that I had ever wanted, every fantasy I had ever dreamed of, every woman I wanted to be with, all flashing before my eyes.

I couldn't take it. I spill my guts, and this is how I'm repaid. I rip my heart out and give it to her to show my undying devotion, and she throws it in my face. Well, if I couldn't have her, no one could. I sold a lot of things for this girl, but the only thing I couldn't part ways with was my 9mm. I pull it out of my trench coat and aim it at her infinitely changing face.

"STOP IT!" I shout.

She stops. I'm shaking, pointing the gun at her; I'm ready to do it. If not for love, then at least to have my life back. Plenty of men have done it before me, killing prostitutes only to dump them in the river. I can be added to the list; I can live with that. As I'm about to pull the trigger, I look at her and realize the form she has taken on.

"...Hannah?" I ask.

Beautiful brown curly hair, dark brown eyes, yoga pants, long red knit sweater, and the most angelic smile. All I can focus on is the smile. The smile of the woman I fell in love with all those years ago. The woman I lost. She died so young. We were teenagers. She just got hit by a car one day, and I never moved on. She was the one. The first one. The first orgasm. The one who sent me on my impossible search, my endless journey. She was my first date, my first kiss, my first blowjob, my first fuck, my first love, my first everything. And then she was gone. But now she's here. The only problem is that I never told this whore that. I told her a lot of things, but I never told her that. I drop the gun in fear, and it thuds to the ground.

"How th— How do you know about Hannah?" I ask

"Come to me, my love. Be with me," she says in her voice. The voice is perfectly recreated.

In a trance, I walk over to her; my legs have a mind of their own. My eyes are glued to her gaze. At this point, I'm crying; I'm in disbelief. It's everything I ever wanted. The hole in my life that has been missing all this time. I walk toward her like a zombie, with a puppy dog grin and tears streaming down my face. And as I get closer, she begins to transform again. Grey hair, blue eyes, mom jeans, plaid shirt.

"Mom?!" I exclaim.

"Yes, sweetheart," she says.

I drift into her arms. I hug her tighter than I've ever hugged anyone before. She still smells of expired scotch and mothballs, her skin is still soft, and she still looks at me with that ever-loving gaze. No matter how much she drank, she was still there for me. She tried her best, and I never resented her for that, even though I act like I do.

"I missed you so much, Mom," I cry.

I know in my head it's not her, but my heart says otherwise.

"I know, honey. But I'm here now. And it's time to come home," she says lovingly.

"What do you mean?" I ask.

As I hug her, I begin to feel myself sinking. Sinking into her. I look to find that I am being absorbed into her like quicksand. Her skin becomes like putty, and the more I fall into her, the more I can feel my skin melting, my bones breaking, my essence fading. All the while her smiling face is looking down on me. She's taking me back. Back home, back to her womb, back to where I truly belong. I manage one last gasp of air before I'm fully eaten alive, and whatever there is of me is now gone from existence.

With a shudder and shake, she digests me whole. She transforms from my mom back into the chubby Asian from before. Then she turns around and leaves the room, closing the door behind her. As she walks down the stairs to the front desk, she's greeted by Al.

"Got another one, baby?" he asks.

"Yes. Yes, I did," she replies.

"Good. I hated that guy," he says.

DAY

140

I was the one who discovered the phenomenon that would be our demise. Two asteroids were going to collide in front of Saggitarius A. What a moment to witness. The effects that it could have and the knowledge we could gain were too great for concern. I pitched the mission to NASA, and they accepted, and soon, a team was put together. I remember them. I remember their names, their faces, who they were. My crew. There were 4 of us. Commander Jacob Brussel, an Air Force Pilot turned astronaut, after his co-pilot crashed their plane into the ocean. He watched the kid die. Winston Jones was an Aerospace Engineer who left his family to die in poverty on the streets of New York and wanted to escape to the stars. Brianna Samson, a Doctor who joined NASA after witnessing the atrocities of WWIII. And me, the Scientist. I got to know them all in time. They were all searching for the same thing: to escape this world. They had all seen the horrors of this Earth and did not want to be a part of it anymore, even if it was just for a short period. The first few days on The Elysian, we hated each other. Jacob was too arrogant, Winston was too serious, Brianna was too kind, and I was too *shy. I kept my distance; I didn't want to form relationships. People from all walks of life, crammed together in the blackness of space with no room for privacy, tend to cause tensions between one another. But we were in this together for something bigger than ourselves. For once in my life, I felt a small semblance of hope.*

"My belly full, my brain at ease, and my heart content."

A HERD OF PIGS

G rocery shopping. I'd rather do it at night: less hassle and fewer people. But I only have time during the day. I go grocery shopping at least once a month. I get my essential fruits and vegetables, I get my toiletries, I get my unhealthy snacks and night-time treats, cold cuts, bread and milk, and coffee. I'm nothing without my coffee. All of those are necessary, but the one thing I cannot live without is pork, or as close to it as you can get. Thankfully, the pigs are never too far from me.

I watch them bounce about the store one by one. I look at their carts to see what they fill their disgusting gullets with. One woman has her cart filled with donuts, microwave dinners, sandwich cookies, and liters of soda. Bad cholesterol, diabetes, and too much fat make for tough meat. But then I pass *him*. The man I've been following for the past few days. I don't even know his name; no need to get personal with the food. They're livestock, nothing more. I watch as he fills his cart with fresh vegetables, fruits, juices, protein powders, and succulent meat. I look over his shoulder and see him scrolling on his phone in his notes app. He has a large list, and he's just getting started. He's going to be here a while, and lucky for me, I've just finished shopping.

I check myself out at the self-service and head to my car to wait for my prey. I never wait in the line. To have the cashier touch my items, to smell them, to hear their snorting and sniveling, I'm afraid I would kill them right then and there. I load my groceries into my car, and I sit on the driver's side, looking towards the entrance. I watch the swine leave with their carts filled. But then I see him leaving. I watch him load the trunk of his car with groceries and then get into his car and drive out of the grocery store parking lot. I then start my engine and begin to follow him to his home. Follow the pig back to his trough.

***

He pulls into the driveway of his suburban home with no garage. I am parked on the street 2 houses down. I've been stalking his house for the past few days. I know he grocery shops around this time, 1 pm. He works from home, so he can do what he likes during the day. His wife is at work, his kids are at school, his neighbors are gone, and the only person around is a sweet elderly woman a few houses down who takes a nap around this time. He is completely alone, and nobody will know he is gone until it's too late. I turn the car on and pull up in front of his house as he is opening his trunk and unloading grocery bags. I step out to greet him, he's thrown off guard, the perfect opportunity.

"Hey there! Mind if I give you a hand?" I ask.

"Uh…no. Do I know you?" he asks in response.

As quickly as the conversation starts, it ends. Hidden in the sleeve of my jacket, I'm holding a hammer by its head while the handle is tucked away within my sleeve. I drop the head so then I can catch it, and in one swift motion, I bash him on the head. He falls to the ground, bleeding profusely. Quickly, I take out a pair of black gloves and put them on.

Can't risk leaving any form of fingerprint or DNA behind. I move back to my car and open the trunk. Then, I scoop him up, holding him in my arms like a baby, and plop him in the trunk, all without getting a single drop of blood on me. I've done this a lot of times; I know what I'm doing. And then it's over. No witnesses, no screams, no sirens, no odors, no trace left behind. Just the faint sound of an old lady snoring, a car engine springing to life, and smooth Jazz on the radio. I leave the scene, making note of how lovely a house he has and what a shame it is to leave so much blood on the driveway.

***

The irony of it all is that I live on a pig farm. It's my bread and butter, raising these pigs to be sold to the likes of the *real* pigs. Have you seen how they treat them? They lasso a rope around them, dragging them through the mud. They fight for their lives, choking them out until their eyes go bloodshot, sniveling and growling for air, until finally they give up. And then three Neanderthal-like men shove them into a trailer. They get dragged off to a meat processing plant, where mechanical drones shoot pressurized bolts into their brains.

I treat my pigs like family. I feed them only the best of food, they have all the room to run around, and when it is time for them to go, I send them off on a warrior's death. I gather all the others around to watch, and as I slit their throat, I say a lord's prayer, and all the pigs squeal for their fallen brothers and sisters. I'd have given this whole operation up a long time ago, but this is all I have, my whole livelihood. Oswaldo and Sons has been in my family for generations. My daddy ran this farm, and his daddy ran it, and his dad before him. And here I am, the last of a generation. Oswaldo the 5th, no wife, no children, just me

85

and the pigs. I pull up to my house on the farm, and I can hear them. My piggies squeal for Daddy. They're hungry, and so am I.

"I know my babies! Give me a couple of hours!" I shout to them.

I open the front door and keep it propped with a brick. Then I go back and open the trunk so I can scoop him up and bring him inside to the kitchen. I lay him out over the large wooden countertop, and I begin to undress him, taking off his shoes, his pants, his shirt, and underwear until he is bare naked. I take the clothes and bring them upstairs to my room. I have a closet full of clothes from different people, with different stories I'll never hear and lives that ended so abruptly. Dresses, slacks, jeans, jumpsuits, dress shoes, boots, sneakers, heels, crop tops, graphic tees, fuzzy socks, fancy socks, all manner of clothes in various sizes and of different tastes. I fold the shirt, bundle the socks, and place them in the appropriate drawers. Then, I hang the pants on the rack and place the shoes with others. I don't have many clothes, so they all fit in my dresser drawers. The same pair of jeans, and the same couple of T-shirts, with the same pairs of boots for most of my life. Now it's time to prep. I go back out to the car and grab the groceries from earlier in the day.

I start by prepping the rub, which consists of Worchester sauce, ketchup, soy sauce, brown sugar, olive oil, garlic cloves, and apple cider vinegar. I mix all of these together in a small bowl. Then, it's time to prep the meat. Under the countertop are drawers filled with all the kitchen utensils and tools I'll need.

First, I grab an electric razor and shave all the hair off of his body, face, and head. I dust them off the counter and place them into the trash can. Then I take out my skinner and skin the man until he is nothing more than a pile of muscle. Starting with the feet and working up from there. I take the skin and hold it up to the light. It's so strange how this flabby mess is what gives us our entire lives. It's what tricks us into believing that we have an identity, that we matter, and that we are somehow more than just animals. I place the skin in a large green trash bin, where soon I will place the rest of the heap. Then I grab my hacksaw and start hacking off the limbs in segments. First, I hack the feet from the ankle, then I cut the shins from the knees, and then the thighs from the torso. Then, I hack the hands from the wrist, the forearm from the elbow, and the biceps from the shoulder blades. And finally, the head from the neck.

Then, it's time to move to the stomach to remove all the internal organs. I take a large knife and make a large incision from the belly button all the way up to the chest. With my bare hands, I pull apart the incision and begin removing the internal organs. The large and small intestine, pancreas, stomach, liver, diaphragm, lungs, and heart. The symbol of love. I place the intestines in the green barrel. Last but not least, the head itself. I take my hack saw and cut the top section of the head, breaking through to the skull. Slowly and carefully, from the wide hole I created, I remove the brain and place it in some Tupperware. I put the head in the barrel with the rest. This whole process is very bloody, so I always make sure to place a large blue tarp on the ground before starting. And when I'm done, I fold it up and place it outside to be hosed down the next morning.

And now it's time to cook. My favorite part is the thigh, a nice thick cut of meat, and less bone to cut through. I'll be having this with the heart and the brain. I take a slice off, and I wash it in the sink, as well as the brain and the heart. I take a fork and start poking holes in the meat. This is so that when I slather the glaze I made earlier, rubbing it into the meat, it will soak up all those juices much easier. Then I put them on a pan that's wrapped in tin foil, and I put them in the oven for 20 minutes at 400 degrees.

While that's cooking, I take the leftover pieces, the dismembered parts, and internal organs and place them into the large green trash bin. It's quite heavy, so I load it onto a small dolly and wheel it outside. I can hear them, my babies. They can smell their supper. Pigs are fascinating creatures. They can't sweat, they're as smart as dogs, and when left starved, they will eat anything. I hate to do it to them, but it's for their own good. They won't eat it otherwise. They just don't understand how good it is for them.

I enter the barn, and they go ballistic. Their squeals could make your ears bleed. You get used to it after a couple of years. The pigs are below the catwalk in 10 pens, five pigs in each pen, each filled with hay and dirt. At the end of the catwalk is a set of switches, which will open each pen and lead the pigs to a large opening that overlooks the catwalk. They can play and frolic, and I can throw them their food. I wheel the barrel up to the edge of the catwalk and pull the switches. The gates open, and the pigs come running. Fifty pigs come barreling down the hallway into their gladiator pit, and I am their Roman emperor. And the thumb is up today my friends.

"Are my little babies hungry?!" I scream.

They squeal in excitement. That means yes.

"Dinner is served!" I yell.

I dump the barrel. Limbs and intestines spill out onto the pigs, and a beautiful rainbow of blood splatters over them. The head comes rolling out last, plopping out like a sacrifice to vengeful gods. The pigs feast, slurping up the intestines like spaghetti; a tug of war with the flesh breaks out between two pigs, and they tear apart the hands and the arms, even breaking the bones with their teeth to get at the bone marrow. They are so damn smart. A bountiful feast for good company. From a distance, I can hear the beeping of the oven. Dinner is ready.

"Eat good, my darlings. Eat good," I say over the sound of munching and crunching.

I get back inside the house, and the food is ready. I grab some oven mitts, take the pan out of the oven, and place it on the stovetop. Cooked to perfection and bubbling with the juices. The sweet smell of Worchester and Garlic hits my nose, and my mouth begins to water. I might have mentioned it earlier, but according to science, pork is the closest thing to the taste of a human. But the way I see it, humans are more animals than pigs. Worse than animals; they're monsters. And that's why I feel no shame, no regret, when I load up my plate with thigh, heart, and brain baked in a Worcester glaze.

I go to the next room and sit down at the kitchen table. My stomach is growling, and I'm so excited I'm shaking a little bit. This is a real treat for me. I only get to do this every couple of months or so just to keep the cops off my trail. To the media, these all look like random kidnappings, and they're only half right. I only choose my victims based on their diet. I scope out grocery stores, checking people's carts for what they eat. Then, I stalk them for a few weeks to get a good idea of their schedule and habits.

There are three grocery stores in my area that I go to: DeMichael's, One Stop, and Food Heaven. I rotate between these three, picking people with healthy diets. Which, believe it or not, is more difficult than you think. Have you seen the way people eat nowadays? Cakes, cookies, frozen dinners, burgers, pizza, super-sized, and extra deep fried. Most people aren't fit for consumption; their insides are rotten, and the meat is spoiled. You are what you eat, after all. But then you find them, the health nuts, the workout geeks, the powerlifters, the bodybuilders, the yoga dorks, the runners, the joggers, and the stretchers; their carts loaded with gluten-free bread, oat milk, vegan pasta, fruits, and vegetables, protein powders, vitamins, and supplements, they keep themselves healthy, their bones strong, their muscles tender, and minimum fat. Perfection. It shows when you take that first bite.

I take my fork and plant it into the "porkchop". Anchored to the plate, I take the knife and cut a nice thin slice. I stab it with my fork and place it into my mouth. It melts, and the flavors pop with each bite. The apple cider vinegar and soy sauce hit first with a sour sting but then quickly become overwhelmed with the sweetness of the brown sugar. The ketchup and Worchester sauce make for a great aftertaste, and the flavors only become more intense with every bite.

Next, I move on to the brain. The brain is a fascinating organ. It controls us; it's what gives us our personality, our identity, our soul; it houses our memories, our hopes and our fears, our dreams and our nightmares. It lets us know when we're hungry, when we're angry, when we're happy, when we're in love, when we're in pain. It's our everything. It also tastes a lot like scrambled eggs. So many crevices, all made for the perfect cut. It's like funnel cake, bite-sized pieces made for grabbing. I picked the surface of the brain with my fingers, then cut it in half and proceeded to eat it with a knife and fork like a gentleman.

Finally, the heart. The heart is our symbol, our expression of love. It pumps the blood that courses through our veins; it beats faster when we're nervous, when we're in love, when we're angry, or when we're afraid. It's our internal compass of how we may navigate through life. I take the fork and knife in my hand, and I go to cut it in half. That's when my more ravenous nature took over, and I grab the heart like an apple and bite into it. As I tear it away, bits of flesh fight to cling on but are too weak for my teeth. A large bite mark has left its imprint, and the veins and ventricles beneath make their appearance.

I savor every bite, taking my time until the plate is clean. When the meal is done, I take my plate and my utensils to the sink. I wash them clean with a sponge and dish soap and then leave them on the rack to dry. I open my front door and yell good night to my piggies. Then I make my way upstairs, where I change into a comfy pair of pajamas. I put my glass of water next to my bedside in case I need it; I turn off my lamp and drift off into a peaceful sleep. My belly full, my brain at ease, and my heart content.

***

The squealing wakes me up. It echoes in the morning air and sends shivers down my spine. I jolt out of bed, and I put on my boots as quickly as I can. I keep my pajamas on, so I don't waste any time. I run down the stairs, bolt through the front door, and sprint as fast as I can across the green to the pig barn.

"My piggies! What's wrong?!" I scream as I enter the barn.

I walk along the center catwalk, looking down into the pens, checking to see if any of them are hurt. But to my surprise…they were gone. All of them. The pens are empty, but I couldn't hear them from outside the barn as I approached. Even as I was opening the door, I could hear it. But once I entered, the sound died as suddenly as it began. The only way they could've got out was if someone hit the switch, opened the gates to the pens, and opened the large barn door in front of the pit that leads outside. But who would do that?

"You've been busy? And here I am, thinking I was first. Humans are so self-centered, aren't we?" said the voice.

I turn around in every direction, quickly looking for the source of the voice, but every shadow, every dark corner, every hidden crevice, every look toward the pens or the open grounds yields no results. Whoever it is, I can't find them.

"Who's there?! Show yourself!" I yelled.

The voice begins to laugh, and that laughter turns into snorting, sort of like one of my pigs.

"You know, if I've done something to you. Take it up with me, not with the pigs. If you've taken them somewhere, just let the pigs go, and I'll give you whatever you want," I begged.

"Tell me: Did they scream? Did they beg? I didn't even get the chance to do anything. Nathan Linklater, 45 years old, and I was the most recent. You just smashed me upside the head, and I was out before I even knew what was happening. But boy, oh boy, did I get to watch the aftermath. I got to watch what you did to me. Then I dug deeper, and I saw what you did to the others. And although some greater force was pulling me into whatever may be, whatever great mystery comes next, I couldn't stand by and let you continue your work. And it seems I wasn't the only one," said Nathan.

Then they came. Out of the shadows. My piggies. They seemed to appear out of nowhere cause I didn't see them before. They scramble out, one by one, circling me around the edges of the catwalk, with me still in the center. Closer and closer, they come, grumbling, snorting, almost giggling.

"My babies, oh, oh my gosh, I thought something had happened to you," I said, concerned.

But they did not respond. Usually, they squeal when they see me, but they just giggle. And still, they slowly inch their way closer to me. A different voice breaks the silence.

"Angela Harrison, you killed me 4 years ago; I was the first. I remember your face back then, so much younger than it is now. So innocent. I've always wondered what it was that broke you that day. Or was it years before, and it just built up over time? Was it a phone call from your mother before she died, telling you how much of a disappointment you are? Or maybe from your father, saying how much of a disgrace you are from the male family line? How about that boy from the diner that you loved so much? Did he call you queer? Maybe it was all of it at once? Honestly, I don't care. All I know is that you took my life away from me. I was only 31; I was young and beautiful. I could've been anyone I wanted. But now I'm stuck like this. In the body of this pig, forever," said Angela.

The pigs. The voices are coming from the pigs. Their mouths don't move, but I can tell. It's like they are projecting their thoughts into my mind, sending shockwaves to my frontal lobe, pulling me into whatever direction they wish. Another voice enters the fray.

"Tommy Matthews, 18 years old, I was the third and the youngest. You could've had anyone that day; why me? My life was just beginning. I didn't even know who I was yet, nor what I could be. But you didn't care. You were just hungry, and I filled your craving," said Tommy.

More voices. All at once, they fill my head, projecting themselves into my brain. A barrage of sorrow and anger, all directed towards me.

"My name is Carly Reagan, killed at my home—"

"Frank Gunner, killed behind the grocery store trying to take a piss—"

"Yensin Tanner, you followed my car and killed me while I stopped to answer a phone call from my wife—"

"Kamala Bedi, you followed me into a truck stop bathroom and slammed my head on the sink—"

My head hurts, my vision spinning. I'm twirling around, trying to get relief when there is none. My knees buckle under the pressure, and I look to the sky for God to save me, but he isn't there. Or he's just really enjoying this.

"STOP!" I scream.

The voices subside, and the pigs disappear. I frantically turn around, looking for any sign of them. Then, I look to the end of the catwalk to find a solitary pig standing at the edge where the controls are.

"It's time for you to pay Oswaldo," said Nathan

"I know," I say.

In a trance-like state, I walk toward him. My arms hang by my side, and my feet drag behind me. I walk past him, walking to the edge of the catwalk. Right to the very edge, and I look down to the dirt pit. My babies are all there, and they're waiting for me. I begin to disrobe myself, removing my shirt, my pants, my shoes, my socks, my underwear, all the way down to my birthday suit. I fold them up neatly and place them off to the side.

"Time for breakfast!" I scream.

And then I leap into the pig's den. I leap, and my heavy body lands hard on the dirt floor and soon the pigs are rushing me. They're stepping on me, kicking me, pounding the meat to make sure it's nice and tender. And then they begin to feast. No skinning, seasoning, sauces, baking, frying, or grilling is required. Pure, unadulterated consumption of flesh and bone. They bite into my skin and muscle, tearing off chunks of thigh and forearm; one of them even bites into my neck. And the whole barn becomes filled with the sound of squealing pigs, snorting and drooling with excitement. Soon, a pool of blood begins to form, soaking into the dirt like a sponge. It splatters all over the pigs, and they proudly roll in their filth. But no matter how bad the pain, I don't fight back. I could never harm my babies, even when they are eating me alive. I look up to see Nathan staring down at me. Even from down here, I can see him smiling.

"Now we can rest," Nathan whispers.

And as the pigs feast on my corpse, the spirits of the poor victims begin to rise out of their pig host bodies. They rise to the sky, being pulled into whatever may be, whatever great mystery comes next.

DAY
365

I remember the day before it happened. We would be at Sagittarius A tomorrow, we would observe the two asteroids, document our findings, and then head home. I remember they were celebrating the mission almost being complete. They were drinking champagne that Winston managed to sneak on board. They asked me to come join them, but I was studying samples of asteroids. Samples similar to that of the asteroids that would be crashing into one another. I wanted to study them further and find anything abnormal in their properties that would cause adverse effects in their collision. I was on the verge of discovery when one of those idiots came crashing into me, knocking over my samples. I would have to begin the work all over again. It was damn Jacob. I pushed him to get away from me, and he replied with a punch to my face. I turned around to look at him, and all I could see was my father.

I threw Jacob to the ground, my hands around his throat. I squeezed and squeezed as hard as I could. Winston was trying to get me off of Jacob, and Brianna was frozen with fear, yelling for me to let go of him. But they could not stop me; my rage was too strong, and when Jacob stopped struggling and his body lay there lifeless, I knew it was over. I let him go, and as soon as I did, Winston pushed me down to the ground and started punching me in the face over and over. Brianna was holding onto Jacob's body, slapping him in the face, hoping that he was unconscious and that he would wake up. But Jacob was dead. I managed to punch Winston hard enough that he lost his focus. I got him off of me and headed toward the lab. I reached for a scalpel that had been sitting with the equipment, and I stabbed Winston multiple times. I could hear the frightful screams of Brianna as she ran off. I got off of Winston's defiled corpse and ran after Brianna. I followed her into the bathroom, and I took care of her just the same.

With my whole crew dead, I shoved their bodies into the escape pod and watched as they flew off into the vastness of space, making their return course back to Earth. When they find the pod crash-landed on the airstrip, they'll find the hopeless remains of the Elysian crew, except for one. I had finally achieved my ultimate goal. To be rid of Earth, to be rid of humanity, and to be alone. I could hijack the ship, override the autopilot, and take it wherever I want in the galaxy. I could travel through another wormhole and end up at any point within the universe. I could find another planet and begin life anew, with different life forms. But call it whatever you want; out of pure curiosity or sheer pride, I left the autopilot on. I wanted to see the asteroids collide into the black hole. After that, the sky was the limit.

"If you love me, then you love yourself. Because we are one and the same."

OUT OF BODY

The driver pulls up to the gate in front of the house. A beautiful German Gothic estate in the middle of the Black Forest, like some German fairytale. For all my mother has done for the country, all the jobs she's provided, all the money she's brought in, I'm pretty sure they'd give her whatever she asked.

The mansion itself is like a big grey stone rectangular box the length of a football field. With windows all around, a stone staircase leading up to the entrance, and a balcony overlooking the luscious green lawn. They had to level a lot of the forest to make this house for her. Mind you, she doesn't do anything with this lawn. It's empty. No lawn ornaments, no designs in the grass, no fountains, no pool; completely devoid of beauty. Just like her.

I had to fly in from California where I'm living. I'm an actress, or at least aspiring. I've done a few commercials, been on some billboards, small parts in movies: Beautiful Dancer #1, Prostitute #3, Stripper #7. Not glamorous parts, I know, but it's something. My mother always thought I would be a doctor or a lawyer or that maybe I would take over the family business. But I wanted nothing to do with my mother. My mother would always say, "Hannah, if you love me, then you love yourself. Because we are one and the same." Then I guess I hate myself because I hate my mother.

Gertrude Gier was the wealthiest woman of her time. Born in 1950, several years after WWII, her family profited well from the genocide of millions, selling out family, friends, and neighbors for societal prestige and selling ammunition to our brothers in the Third Reich. When Gertrude became of age she inherited the family fortune and the empire that came with it. But to be fair to my mother, she did not share her family's sentiments and spent the rest of her life transforming Gier Industries from a weapons manufacturer to Hochburg Autos, one of the biggest automotive companies in the world. She moved the company to America and transitioned from being a cold-hearted Nazi to a cold-hearted capitalist. She was known for her crude demeanor and her lack of empathy or understanding; she would often talk down to her employees, created harsh working conditions, and there were even a few worker strikes. But she made money, and that's all that mattered to the shareholders. Her company created the Kraftwagen sports car, one of the highest-selling German cars in America. Hochburg, named after Hochburg Castle. It's located near the village of Sexau, where she grew up. And near the village of Sexau is Schwarzwald. The Black Forest.

My father told me all about the Black Forest. The Romans gave it that name for its strangely dark-hued trees. The forest is so thick and dense that light has a hard time reaching the ground floor. And as these things tend to happen, many strange things occur in those woods. Everything from vampires, werewolves, dwarves, trolls, and ghosts, there's even the story of King Mummelsee at the bottom of Mummel Lake with his army of lady sirens. They lure in travelers with their beautiful singing and drag them to the bottom of the lake for the king to feast upon. But more feared than any were the witches. Some say Hansel and Gretel were victims of a witch in the Black Forest, as told by the Brothers Grimm. My father always used to say that my mother was a witch. She would get all mad and flustered, and my father would always laugh it off. Well, it wasn't that funny to me. For all I knew, she really was a witch. She sure as hell acted like it. And not just to everyone else.

When I was 8 years old, she started making me take diet pills; I would have to track my meals, she made me weigh myself every day, and I wasn't allowed to eat lunch at school, only breakfast and dinner. When I was 13, she would do my make-up every morning before school, along with an assortment of creams and ointments. When I was 16, she made me join the track team, and she would wake me up on the weekends and make me run a mile. I would be crying, begging her to take me home, but she would look at me from the bleachers with scorn. To her, I was a little rag doll, her plaything that she could mold and shape to her liking. My mother had a lot of issues. My therapist told me that my mother probably had a lot of generational trauma, that she felt guilty for the sins of her family and what the Nazis did. Her behavior towards her employees, her friends and family, and me is her way of keeping absolute control over things. Whatever. Honestly, I think she's just a bitch. I think that evil is there, tucked away inside of her. Generation upon generation of evil, just waiting to be let loose. My father died over a decade ago, and soon after, she retired. I guess she had grown tired of America, and decided to settle herself back in Germany. And she set up shop in the middle of the Black Forest.

My mother gave the driver a key to the gate, so he had to get out of the car and open the gate himself. He pulls the gate open and gets back into the car, and we drive down the dirt road that leads up to the green lawn. My mother didn't want the dirt road leading to the entrance. She would prefer her guests walk up the hill leading to the stone steps. She would relish in watching them break a sweat, it would make them weak, catch them off guard, while she held all of the superiority.

I tip the chauffeur and thank him for a lovely drive. He tips his hat to me, and he drives away. I'm jealous. I'd rather have that old man stare me up and down for another hour than deal with what is about to come. I hike up the slightly hilled green lawn and walk up those blasted stone steps. By the time I grab the gold metal knocker and pound upon the door, I'm sweating and breathing heavily. The knock echoes through the woods, almost like a beckoning call to the dark forces hiding behind the trees.

An old woman, 5 feet 5 inches, 2 inches shorter than me, with the deepest of wrinkles you've ever seen on her cheeks and forehead. Her face is in a constant contortion of anger and disappointment. Her teeth are yellow, the skin on her neck is sagging, her hair is as grey as cremated remains, purple blotches on her arms, and the skin is so thin it's wrapped to the bone. She is wearing a traditional German dress, with a brown corset and a blue bottom with red flowers. Underneath that, she is wearing a white dress shirt, white dress pants, and black boots. My mother.

"What are you wearing?" she said in a strong German accent.

The first thing out of her mouth. She hasn't seen me in over 10 years, her own daughter, and she can't even muster a "Hello sweetheart!" As to what I am wearing, I'm wearing a large beige American-made workman jacket, unintentionally ripped jeans with ketchup stains on them, and old black boots that have seen better days. I wore this because I knew that my mother wouldn't approve. I have this naive hope that my mother will one day just accept me for who I am. That she will just change overnight, and she will regret all of the harmful things she's done to me. But it never happens, and I get moments like this.

"It's just what I'm wearing, Mother. Are we going to do this now? I just got here," I retorted.

"I will give you the number of my stylist. Come in," said my mother.

I enter into the mansion, and the nightmare begins. Walking through the halls, I'm hit with the all-too-familiar stench of dust, mold, and rust. I've said a lot about my mother, enough to make anyone want to run away screaming in terror. But one thing I failed to mention is that she is somewhat of a…hoarder. If you asked her, she would say collector, but to collect would imply some sort of method to the madness, some sort of semblance of organization, interest, and taste. But that's not the case.

Her house is filled with Greek statues, expensive guitars, collections of antique spoons, knives owned by serial killers, forks owned by royalty, bookshelves filled with books on the occult never opened, as well as all the classics of literature, thousands of Russian dolls, Roman gold coins, Hindu scrolls, Ming dynasty vases, Faberge eggs, expensive comic books, Nazi memorabilia and unknown metals purchased from unspecified government agencies. She doesn't even sleep in the master bedroom, floor to ceiling is all clothing from around the world, of the highest and best material. Blouses, dresses, pants, shirts, sweatshirts, cardigans, sweaters, jackets, boots, sneakers, dress shoes, and even men's clothing from when my father was alive.

I swear, sometimes the place feels bigger on the inside than it does on the outside. Go further down the hall, through Greek stone archways, and you'll find a warehouse filled with every car ever conceived, every boat, every motorcycle, every bicycle, unicycle, pogo stick, scooter, skateboard, any mode of transportation, my mother has it. Stashed away, never to be touched, never to be ridden. Rusting away, parts becoming stale, gears turning dry, and cobwebs forming. Behind the house is the above-ground pool, next to the below-ground pool, next to the trampoline. On the outskirts of the property is an entire zoo of exotic and unexotic animals. You have your dogs and your cats, your lions and leopards, crocodiles and alligators, tucans and pigeons, buffalo and cows, sheep and pigs.

The only thing she's never owned is a human, but Hilda is about as close as she could get to that. Hilda is the maid, but she gave up cleaning the house years ago. My mother will tell her to clean, and Hilda will tell her she already did, and my mom believes her every time. My mother tricked Hilda when she was 18 into signing a contract of employment, and whenever the contract expires, my mother's lawyer is somehow able to extend the end date. That was 40 years ago now; an indentured servant, Hilda, will most likely work for my mother till the day she dies.

To much surprise, nobody has tried to rob this house in the 10 years or so my mom has lived here. Then again, nobody comes here. Who would dare enter the enchanted Black Forest? Plus, my mom didn't exactly make many friends throughout her life, nor did she invite anyone truly into her life. My father was the exception. Otto Gier was the love of her life. He was the only one who seemed to understand, who knew how to calm her down, how to deal with her tantrums, to make her cry, to make her laugh, and to make her smile. He saw something that no one else could see. What was it? Beats me. It must've been buried deep, deep, deep down inside her because nobody could see it. He died from cancer; she had to watch him die slowly, painfully. I think it truly did break her, and it's probably the only time I truly felt sorry for my mother. I didn't understand her; no one understood her, but he did. And that's what matters. But he's gone, and she's all alone.

"I see the *collection* is growing. Or is it? I can't tell. It all just looks like a pile of shit to me," I remarked.

"It's nothing compared to the piles of shit you've been eating in America. I can see your tummy rolls from here, sweetheart," she replied.

"The only rolls here are the rolls of skin flapping from your neck, you little T-Rex," I retorted.

"Please, if anyone's a T-Rex, it's you with that rashy skin of yours," she insulted.

"Dinner is served," Hilda suddenly said, stopping me from decking my mother in the face.

Hilda leads us to the dining room, which is about the size of a small army base, with a table about half that size. Cartoonishly long, like something you would see in a Medieval king's castle, my mother placed on one end and me on the other. There are only two chairs, one on each end. My mother takes the chair closest to us, so I have to trek across the length of the table just to get to the other side. By the time I sit down in my chair, I feel like I've just run a marathon. From the kitchen, Hilda brings in a tray of Rouladen, a traditional German dish consisting of pickles and bacon wrapped in thin slices of beef, served with gravy, mashed potatoes, and cabbage. Hilda places a plate on my mother's side, then hikes across the room to my side and places my plate down.

Now, you're probably asking yourself, "If you hate your mother so much, why are you visiting her?"

Because she's dying of breast cancer. I got checked myself before I came here, just to make sure. I'm as healthy as a horse for now. In her will, she has decided to leave me everything. The entire Gier empire, mine to inherit, all the money and all of her crap that comes along with it. So I'm here to sign some papers, talk to some lawyers, and get what's coming to me.

"So, how are the dope fiends and pedophiles treating you in California?" asked my mother.

"Not as bad as the ghosts, goblins, and witches lurking in the Black Forest. Honestly, Mother, I don't understand why you moved out here," I said as I shoved food in my face.

As much as I hate to admit, the food is good. It reminds me of my childhood, of simpler times. On the few days when my mother was generous, she would make this dish for me. It's one of the rare good memories I have.

"They keep me company, unlike some people. So, I suppose we should get down to business," said my mother, not even touching her food.

She snaps her fingers, and in comes Hilda, holding a manilla folder with some papers in it and a pen hooked onto the folder. She hands them to my mother, who slides them across the table and perfectly lands in front of my plate.

"I promise I'll take good care of the family business," I said.

Which is a lie. I plan on hiring someone to run the company while I reap all the benefits. With all that money, I'll be able to start my acting career. I'll be able to get into the fanciest parties, sleep with the wealthiest men, and star in *real* movies. My life will finally begin. I grab the folder and open it up, looking over the necessary documents. I sign on the dotted lines with my signature, and the deal with the devil is complete. I slide the papers back over to my mother, and they land in front of her plate. Hilda snatches them up and walks off back into the kitchen.

"Oh, I'm sure you will. Honestly, Hannah, I expected more from you, " my mother chided.

"So did I," I said, chewing through my food.

Just then, I noticed a weird taste, something akin to dish soap. I was so hungry and angry that it took me a second to realize the room was spinning, my temperature rising, and my legs getting woozy.

"Mom, what did y—" I try to say. But as I go to stand up, I lose balance completely, and I fall to the ground. I can't move; I'm too weak.

"Are you okay, sweetheart? You really should take better care of yourself. I mean, look at you. The first bite of a home-cooked meal and your fainting. Oh, wait! It must've been those drops of GHB that I had Hilda put in the Rouladen. Silly me!" explained my mother.

I catch the last sentence my mother spoke before my vision goes black, and I am completely unconscious.

***

I awake in the darkness of the Black Forest. I'm disoriented at first, weak and frail. But I manage to lift my slumped-over head and ever so slowly open my eyes. I open them to find that I am naked, tied to a tree, my arms and legs immobilized. And it's not till then that I notice the massive, raging fire. And she's there too, my mother. Naked as well, dancing around the giant bonfire, the flames almost reaching the heavens. I try to scream, but my mouth is gagged. I can only slam my head against the tree trunk in frustration as I watch my mother contort her body in unnatural ways, her breasts swaying back and forth, her hair flowing in the breeze.

I hear a muffled scream off in the corner, similar to my own. I look over, and another woman has been tied up and gagged. She lays on the ground, ropes tied around her ankles and knees, her hands tied behind her back, rope wrapped around her body and her arms. I recognize her; it's Hilda. I try to wriggle myself free, anything I can do to get out of my bonds, anything to try to help her, but it's no use. She wriggles around on the ground like a worm, looking for wet earth, but no matter how hard she tries, she only finds solid concrete.

In our struggle, we failed to notice that my mother had stopped dancing, and she was watching us. Against the flamelight, she looked as ominous as could be. The shadows hid most of her twisted features, and only some were illuminated by the flame. Her evil smile glinting off the orange light might as well have come from the devil himself. Slowly, she walked herself over to Hilda. For a woman her age, I was not expecting her to display such feats of strength; for her, she was able to pick up Hilda with no problem whatsoever. She picked Hilda up and lifted her over her body, holding her high in the air like she was some newborn toddler. My mother carried her body over to the bonfire and threw her in. The gag had been burned away, and her screams were in full force. Hilda screamed and screamed like a banshee, but they fell on deaf ears. I watched as her body charred and burned, skin peeling off, bones cracking, and soul departing.

At the gruesome sight, a stream of urine trickled down my leg, like I was a little schoolgirl. Once my mother was finished, she turned around and walked over to me. I could see her more closely now; the light was gone from her eyes. Any semblance of human was gone as if her essence had been stripped away as if something took hold of her. She had hold of a knife; it seemed to appear out of nowhere, and she cut her hand with it. She then took her bloody hand and smeared it all across my face. She took both hands and clasped onto my head, and she began to chant in German:

"Dunkle Mächte, ich rufe dich an. Schenke mir ewiges Leben."
"Dark forces, I call upon you. Grant me eternal life."

Over and over again, she chanted this. It went on for minutes before they appeared. Demons. Hundreds of tiny little demons appeared out of the shadows, out of the corners of my eyes, behind my mother, and behind every tree, hundreds of little demons. They didn't look like what I had imagined. Little blobs of animated shadow, with claws and spindly arms and legs, their eyes like twinkling stars in the night sky. They had one singular horn like a mohawk on their head, and they had the sharpest of teeth. Hundreds of them encroach upon me and my mother. Slowly and slowly, they came for us, taking all the time in the world. I couldn't have been more terrified, but not my mother. She seemed to embrace the creatures, awaiting whatever ill intent they might have.

They climbed on us. Some were crawling up the tree, while others were crawling down from the tree. They climbed all over me, groping me, laughing while they did so. They did the same to my mother, but she did so with outstretched arms and a look of pure ecstasy on her face. Then, they began to climb inside us. They didn't rip us apart, but rather, they just sank into us like a ghost would. Each one climbed into my belly, and with each one felt like a cannonball ripping through me. One after the other, after the other, after the other. Again, my mother seemed to enjoy this. With every one, she seemed to be having the greatest pleasure she could ever experience. I tried to scream, but the pain was so alarming it took my breath away.

Soon, the ones who entered would exit, and they would switch over from one body to the other. They would exit my mother and enter into me, then from me into my mother. And they did this for what felt like hours, but with the intensity of the pain, who really knows how long it was. Between their trips, I could vaguely make out something they were carrying. Little glowing white orbs, some sort of essence. But I couldn't tell. Soon, the pain became too much, and slowly, my vision began to fade once more. The fire began to die out, and darkness was encroaching upon me. The last thing I saw was my mother's euphoric face. And it was the strangest thing, for with each passing second, her face was becoming mine. Slowly, her features were morphing and changing into mine. My eyes were staring back into mine, and then I passed out.

***

My vision comes back. I try to move, but I am frozen. I can't move my head, my arms, or my legs, and I can't even move my mouth. My arms are to the side, and I am standing up straight. I don't even know where I am; the only thing I do know is that I seem to be in a glass case, like some doll on display. I'm in a room I've never seen before. And to my surprise, it's completely empty. None of my mother's junk, nothing at all. Except for her and I.

"You won't be able to move sweetheart. You're frozen in place and in time. You will stay there until you die of the cancer that once inflicted me," said my mother.

I hear her voice off in the distance, but I can't see her. Then she walks into eyesight, and I can't believe what I'm seeing. I have to blink several times, but it always stays the same. She's wearing a large beige American-made workman jacket, unintentionally ripped jeans with ketchup stains on them, and old black boots that have seen better days. I wore this because I knew that my mother wouldn't approve. And now she's wearing it. And she's wearing my face.

"No, your eyes do not deceive you. You are me, and I am you," she says from below me.

Impossible. There's no way. It must be the GHB, making me hallucinate, my mind playing tricks on me. The whole thing must've been a dream. The woods, the fire, Hilda, the demons; some twisted illusion put upon by my mother. But then I saw the book she was holding in her hands. It was covered in symbols unrecognizable to me and written in a language unknown to humankind. I could feel its evil, its demonic energy.

"A book I found admist my collection. I discovered a ritual to transfer my soul to the body of another. Therefore, ridding me of my illness and old age and passing it along to another," explained my mother.

I use every ounce of my willpower to try and move, to wriggle, to kick, to punch, to scream, anything to awake from this horrible dream. But it is no use. The only thing I can manage to do is to drop a single tear down my cheek.

"All it required was a measly human sacrifice. Shame about poor Hilda. But now I'm you, Hannah. Hannah Gier just inherited the enormous fortune of her late, great mother. Having inherited said fortune, she will no longer pursue her ridiculous dream of acting and will instead run the Hochburg Auto company as was always intended. I really must thank you, Hannah. Out of all of the things I've owned in my life, the only thing I've never been able to own is myself. And now I have you, forever trapped in my glass case, my sleeping beauty," my mother finishes.

And with that, she begins to walk away. I can hear her boots stomping as she closes the door, leaving me behind to rot in an old, aging body for the rest of my days. But not before she turns around to me one last time.

"You know, perhaps I shall begin a new collection. This room needs to be filled with something, and there are lots of pretty girls in the world," says my mother as she closes the door.

My mother used to say, "Hannah, if you love me, then you love yourself. Because we are one and the same."

???

I'm in a jail cell. The grey concrete walls are on all four sides, and I can see the guards through the metal bars. I'm wearing standard orange prison garb, and I am lying in my bed, hooked up to high-tech machinery. There's a heart monitor and a tube filling me with god knows what. I am old, I am wrinkly, and I am pathetic. After Elysian landed, I was arrested for the murders of my crew. I was brought to trial and sentenced to life in prison. I watch as I draw my final breath, and the lights leave my eyes. And the lavender plant wilts and dies, sending a tribe of dust into the orange sky above me, and green energy pulsating beneath my feet.

I decided to walk and try to find the end. The end of all things. The end of the Lavender Fields. I couldn't find it. I walked and walked for what felt like several days, and I always ended up back in the same spot. I walked in the opposite direction, and I would end up in the same spot in a matter of hours. I would turn left and walk back around in minutes. I would turn right, and walk back around in seconds. Every variation would lead me back to the same spot over and over.

I understand now. I see it. A clock without a craftsman. A field without a gardener. Time is linear to us; that's how we experience it. But in reality, it's happening all at once, all at the same time. It's always happening, it's always ending, and it's always beginning. Something didn't come from nothing, something is just always happening. It's all in a perpetual motion, with no cause, that will never end. It will all be happening again and again, with different people, at different times, in different galaxies, in different universes, in different dimensions. And it all means nothing. No grand design, no purpose to be fulfilled. Let this be my final testament. My written word. My warning: All is not as it seems, for there was nothing there to begin with.

ACKNOWLEDGMENTS

I'd like to give thanks to Kayleigh Sorrentino, my partner in crime, who suffered through reading the first drafts of these stories. And through what I can only describe as magic, created illustrations that perfectly capture the essence of these stories.

A special shout-out deserves to go to the staff at Omar's World of Comics, my day-job, who have supported my writing journey. They are a special kind of work place and have nurtured my love for writing and storytelling.

Of course, I have to thank my family. My parents and my brother have been my biggest supporters since the day I was born. Always supporting me through whatever creative endeavor I decided to embark on, always pushing me to work harder, always cheering me on to the finish line.

And finally, I have to thank *you*. Thank you for bothering to pick this book up and give it a shot. Thank you for being a part of my journey, and for helping me one step at time, as I achieve my writing dream.

Thank you!

ABOUT THE AUTHOR:

Derek Mola was born and raised in Massachusetts, graduating from Emerson College, with a degree in Visual Media Production. Tired of the film industry, he became obsessed with horror and fantasy short stories and set out to write his own. His first novel is *Anansi's Web*, a collection of short dark fantasy stories.

Derek Mola   @mola.derek   @derek.mola

https://www.derekmola.com/

Made in the USA
Columbia, SC
26 October 2024

44685824R00067